BURNED

SHADOWS OF THE VOID BOOK 6

J.J. GREEN

BOOKS ORDER

The Books of Shadows of the Void - Complete Series

Prequel: Starbound
Book 1: Generation
Book 2: Stranded
Book 3: Dawn
Book 4: Shadowrise
Book 5: Underworld
Book 6: Burned
Book 7: Trapped
Book 8: Mars Born
Book 9: Shadow Battle
Book 10: Shadow War
Books 1 - 3 The Galathea Chronicles
Books 4 - 7 The Earth Chronicles
Books 8 - 10 The Galactic Chronicles

1
———

Jas was having a staring competition with the Minister for Global Security. She had locked eyes with the long-haired, kaftan-wearing government official, who was tied to a rickety wooden chair. Above them both, a single bare light strip illuminated the windowless basement room. Jas wasn't up to speed on the politics and politicians of Earth's Global Government—her brief visits to Earth between deep space missions didn't allow for it—but she'd been told the woman's name was Bathsheba Dubois, and that she'd been in office for three and a half years.

Three and a half years was plenty long enough for her to have been killed and replaced by a Shadow—a perfect copy of the victim, only inhabited by a hostile alien. What Jas had to find out was simple: was it the real Bathsheba sitting before her, or was it Shadow Bathsheba? If she was the actual Minister, Jas and her friends were guilty of the crime of kidnapping. But if it was a Shadow, Jas was one step closer to alerting the Transgalactic Council that Earth was gradually being infected and taken over by an alien menace.

Bathsheba was the first to crack. She broke her stare, and her eyes shifted to the side. Jas gave a slight nod of satisfaction. The minister seemed to be weakening a little, and now she might respond to questioning. As part of her training as a security officer Jas had learned how to interrogate effectively, but she didn't want to employ the harsher methods she knew. She had a distaste for them, and there was a chance the woman sitting before her was a human being.

"How did you know it was me in the car?" Bathsheba asked.

Jas straightened up in surprise. After removing her gag, she'd endured longer than an hour of furious threats and demands from the minister. Her question was the first real attempt at communication she'd made.

The truth was, Jas hadn't known she was kidnapping a Global Government minister when she'd attacked her limousine. She'd been trying to kidnap another, known, Shadow. Unsure of the wisdom of giving away that information, Jas replied, "It wasn't easy. You all travel in identical unmarked limousines. Maybe you should think about updating your security policy in that area."

Bathsheba shrugged. "A motorcade only draws attention to important officials. And these days, when a targeted airstrike from kilometers away is technically easy to arrange, anonymity is the best defense. It's worked pretty well."

"Until now."

Another shrug. "Security must be constantly revised and updated as threats develop and evolve."

She was stating one of the first principles Jas had ever learned. Bathsheba Dubois was no lightweight. She knew her stuff. But her statement wasn't evidence that she was the real Bathsheba. The longer Shadows spent living as replicants of their victims, the more they unlocked their memories and knowledge, and the more like them they became. Jas had heard that some Shadows even became confused about who they were, eventually.

What information could she get from the woman that would clearly identify her? Shadow Bathsheba could probably answer any question the original Bathsheba could. A certain emptiness behind the eyes or a vagueness in the gaze were some signs of a recently created Shadow replacement, but the woman showed neither of those symptoms.

"So," said Bathsheba, "what's your organization? What are you demanding for my return? You realize that the police are homing in on this location as we speak? You know, if you give yourselves up now, before it's too late, you might be spared the death penalty."

"Are you trying to tell me you've been fitted with a tracker?" asked Jas. "That's a lie. They would have been here a long time ago if that were the case. Don't worry. I know all about trackers. No. No one knows where you are. No one's ever going to find you."

Bathsheba's gaze wavered. Her anger had given way to fear, Jas detected, though the woman was trying to hide it. *Good.* Maybe she would reveal something that would give away her true identity. "Tell me what you know about Shadows," she said, watching the minister's expression closely.

Surprise flickered over her face but was quickly suppressed. "What a ridiculous question. Shadows are shade cast by objects standing in light."

Jas's lips thinned. "Don't waste my time and yours. You know what I mean. You know what Shadows are. The Government's been covering them up long enough. You've been pretending to the Transgalactic Council that you have the situation under control, and you've suppressed all reports about them in the media. But they're here, and they're taking over. You've let the situation get out of hand. Or maybe your victim did."

"Wait. You think I'm a Shadow?" Bathsheba sat upright. "Is that what this is about? That's why you kidnapped me? But that doesn't make any sense. You could have informed the vidnews channels if you really thought that. You could have—"

"Told the media you've silenced?"

Bathsheba paused. Her shoulders sagged. It seemed the natural reaction of someone in her position, but it could also be the mimicry of a Shadow.

"I'm not a Shadow," said Bathsheba. "I don't know how to prove it to you, but I'm not. Listen. If you know about them and you're fighting them, we're on the same side. Protecting Earth from Shadows is the Global Government's number one task. The longer you keep me here, the closer we come to losing that fight. You have to let me go so I can do my job."

Jas snorted. "From what I've seen, we stand a better chance without you in power."

Her face reddening, the minister replied, "You have no idea what you're talking about. You have no idea the lengths I've gone to in order to fight this menace."

Jas stepped closer and bent down so that her face was inches from Bathsheba's. "The tests you use aren't working. Shadows are flooding onto the planet. The parents of a very good friend of mine have gone missing, probably taken by Shadows. There are Shadows in the refugee institutions. There are Shadows in your own offices. Whatever lengths you've gone to, they *aren't enough*."

Behind her, the door opened. It was Sayen, looking tired and in pain. Less than a day ago, she'd had an operation to remove a tracking device her parents had placed in her. The wound had to be sore.

"You," gasped Bathsheba, her eyes widening. "Then you aren't a Shadow. I thought not when I interviewed you, but when you disappeared..."

"No, I'm not," Sayen replied. "Can I talk to you?" she asked Jas, who followed her outside.

"Erielle still isn't back," she said, after Jas closed the door. "It's nearly dusk. She should have been here hours ago. Something must have gone wrong. She's been captured, or hurt. Maybe she's stuck at the Security HQ, Jas, and she can't get out. Maybe she's unconscious, and she needs our help. She's covered in invisibility spray. How are we ever going to find her?" Sayen's voice had been rising as she spoke, and her lower lip trembled.

"Let's go upstairs." Jas locked the door and helped Sayen mount the steps to the first floor. The missing underworlder leader hadn't escaped her mind, but she wasn't sure what they could do. The last they'd heard, it had sounded like she was in great danger. Since then, the radio contact they had with her had been silent, even when they'd risked hailing her. But they couldn't storm the Global Government Security Headquarters. They didn't have the firepower. And even if they managed to get inside, what then? They had no clue where she might be.

But Sayen and Erielle were lovers, and Jas didn't want to crush her hopes that the underworlder might still turn up alive and well. "We'll talk to her people and see what they suggest. They must be just as worried as we are. How's Makey doing?"

"He sleeps most of the time, but he seems to be getting better. I dressed his wound. It's healing up."

"That's great. Why don't you go back to your room, and

I'll talk to the underworlders about Erielle. Do you know where Carl is?"

"He said he was going to get some sleep, but that was a while ago."

"Okay, thanks. You try to sleep, too, and try not to worry. We'll do our best to find Erielle. I promise."

Leaving Sayen in the underworlders' medical treatment room, Jas went to find Carl. The pilot was alone in the communal bedroom. He was lying on his back, but he was awake. His hands behind his head, he was staring out the window into the twilight. He looked sad and wistful. Jas wondered if he was thinking about his missing parents.

"Carl?" she said, breaking him from his reverie.

He sat up. "Did you find out if that woman's a Shadow?"

Jas shook her head.

"Krat."

"I don't know how we're going to know for sure. But that isn't what's on my mind at the moment. Would you come with me to talk to the underworlders about Erielle?"

"She still not back?"

"No, and none of them seem to be doing anything about it."

"That's not good."

The building was strangely empty and quiet. They didn't find Erielle's followers until they'd climbed right to the top, where her private rooms were. When they went in, they found all the underworlders gathered there. A meeting was going on, but silence fell abruptly the moment Jas and Carl showed their faces.

"Something we can do for you?" asked a large man, who appeared to have been addressing the rest. His tone was sarcastic. Jas recognized him as one of the men who had accompanied Erielle and Sayen when they had stolen the blood that saved Makey's life.

"I think you all agree Erielle has to be in trouble," Jas said. "If you have a plan for some way to find her, we'd like to help."

"What a generous offer," said the man. "But, sorry, whatever we decide to do, your *help* won't be needed."

2

———

J as rattled the padlock on the cabinet. It was a simple mechanical device, typical of the underworlders' dislike and distrust of technology. Luckily for Jas, that meant it would also be simple to break. She lifted up the blaster she was holding, preparing to hit the lock with its handle.

"I'm not sure this is a good idea," said Carl, grabbing her arm before she could bring it down.

"Carl, if the underworlders turn against us, we won't stand a chance unless they're unarmed." But her friend's worries made her pause. They both looked at Erielle's weapon cabinet while they decided what to do.

"When they find out we stole their guns," Carl said, "they're definitely gonna turn against us." He let go of her arm.

"You saw that guy at their meeting. He was talking them into throwing us out, or worse. And what are we going to do then? Sayen can barely walk, and Makey's too sick to move. Who knows what they'll do with the minister we kidnapped." She sighed. "I agree it might turn out not to be the best move, but in our current situation, I don't think we have a choice. Offense is the best defense."

After the underworlder's rejection of their offer to help them find their leader, the rest of them had stared at Jas and Carl in silence until they left. Whatever they thought of the large man's comments, it was clear that the underworlders still thought of them as outsiders. Their presence at Erielle's place was on very shaky ground. Jas knew she would feel a whole lot more comfortable with their weaponry under her control.

Carl seemed to have run out of arguments. "I suppose you're right. Go ahead."

Jas raised her blaster again and brought the hard edge of the handle down on the lock. The metal rings on the door that held the lock bent, but they didn't break. Jas tried again, but the welding held firm. The lock was turning out to be a lot tougher than antique vids implied. She would have to blast it.

She turned the weapon in her hand and aimed it before delivering a short beam. It sizzled the metal, and the lock clanked as it hit the floor. Erielle's cabinet of wonders opened before them. She had a variety of weapons in there. Jas was familiar with most of them, though some were so old she'd only ever seen pictures of them.

They hastily filled a bag with the cabinet's contents. They didn't know how long the underworlders' meeting would go on. Jas was worried about Makey and Sayen lying unprotected in the medical center.

Soon, the cabinet shelves were empty, and their bag was bulky and heavy. Its weight didn't reassure Jas, however. With their criminal connections, the underworlders would have few problems replenishing their supply. Stealing Erielle's stock was, at most, only buying them a little time.

"That it?" Carl asked, leaning over Jas's shoulder to peer into the dark recesses of the cupboard.

"Yeah, we've got everything."

"Krat."

"What's wrong?"

"Where's the invisibility spray?"

Jas's heart sank. "You're right. It isn't here. I swear Erielle put it back before we left for the security HQ. Someone's taken it already."

"Yeah. Someone's thinking ahead. Probably that fella who was running the meeting."

"Nothing we can do about it now. We've got everything else. Looks like I was right to be cautious. Let's get downstairs to the medical center."

Both Sayen and Makey were in bed but awake when Jas and Carl appeared with their cache of weaponry. Carl explained what had been said at the underworlders' meeting, and neither of them was slow to understand the danger they were in.

"Jas, did you get anywhere questioning the minister?" Sayen asked.

"Well, once she stopped cussing me out and started talking...I don't know. Either she's doing a good job of acting like the real Bathsheba Dubois, or she isn't a Shadow."

Sayen grimaced. "I really thought she was. She was so cold toward me. And the fact that she was interviewing all the job applicants, it seemed like she was trying to assess me to see if I was worth turning into a Shadow."

"I think she might have been interviewing candidates herself because she was worried about Shadows infiltrating the department," said Jas. "She was trying to check for them."

Sayen shook her head. "Things must have gotten really bad. We've got to do something."

"Of course, and we're trying," Jas said. "But it looks like our plan of catching a Shadow has failed again. We still don't have anything to convince the Transgalactic Council that Earth's politicians have been lying."

The door flew open and banged against the wall. The underworlder who had been addressing the meeting stood in the doorway, and the space behind him was crowded.

"We've come to a decision," said the man. "You can stay one more night, then you're all to leave first thing in the morning. Erielle's not coming back from the look of it. You guys were only ever here because she wanted it. No one else did. We've lost friends because of you. You're bad luck, and you're trying to drag us into a fight that's none of our business. If it were up to me, you'd be out of the door right now, but some people feel sorry for the kid. So we've agreed, you've got one more night. In the morning, you can pack up your stuff and get out."

"We can't leave in the morning," exclaimed Sayen. "Makey isn't nearly well enough yet. He almost died. He can't just get up and leave."

"Look…" said the man, approaching Sayen until he was within a few inches of her.

Jas slowly reached inside the bag of weapons, which the man seemed to have mistaken as containing their belongings.

"I could've died or gotten arrested stealing blood for that kid," he continued. "And why? He isn't one of us. He's a complete stranger. I only did it because Erielle asked me to. But now she's gone, and we're going to see a few changes around here."

Jas wondered if those changes included him taking over

in Erielle's place. He was standing only a short distance from the petite navigator. With her enhancements, she could take care of herself, but Jas didn't want him thinking he could bully them into doing whatever he wanted.

"You're crowding my friend," she said. "Leave us alone. We've heard what you have to say, and we'll talk about it. If it suits us to leave in the morning, we'll go."

The underworlder lifted a corner of his mouth. "You're going whether you agree to it or not," he said. But he moved back. "I'll be back at dawn." Pushing against them with his broad frame, he broke through the other underworlders who were peering in through the door, following the proceedings with great interest.

Carl closed the door on their curious faces and leaned his back against it. A tense pause followed. "Hey, Jas, give me a hand with this," he said, indicating a tall metal cupboard full of medical equipment. Together, they positioned the cupboard in front of the door. It wasn't much of a barricade, but the door didn't have a lock and it was the best they could do.

"I'm sure I'll be well enough to move in the morning," Makey said. The kid's appearance belied his words. He was pale, and the bones of his face were clearly outlined beneath his skin.

"Even if you were," Jas said, "which you're not, we aren't going anywhere. We've kidnapped a government minister. The minute anyone in the street sees her, the game's over for us. And where would we go? We don't have any creds to pay for a place to stay."

"That's not strictly true," Sayen said. "Do you remember the first time we tried to kidnap a Shadow, Erielle gave us a map showing us a safe, empty house. She said we could stay there a while. I've still got the map."

"You do?" said Jas. "That's great, but I don't think we should move until you're both well enough, and maybe not until we decide what to do with the minister."

"What *are* we going to do with her?" Sayen asked.

"Krat knows."

A shout came from upstairs, followed by the rumble of many feet running down toward them.

"Looks like they found out about their weapons," said Carl.

"What weapons?" Sayen asked.

Jas opened the bag she was carrying. Sayen's eyebrows rose, and her mouth fell open as she looked inside.

3

Jas and Carl had their backs to the cupboard they'd put in front of the door, and their legs were braced against the floor. Incoherent shouting was coming from outside, and the cupboard rattled as the underworlders tried to break through. Jas pushed back as hard as she could, but her feet began to slide across the floor as the door was slowly forced open.

"Kratting digifreaks. Give us our weapons back," shouted a deep voice. "Thieves," called another. "Erielle should never have let you in. You've been nothing but trouble since you first showed your faces." "Open up," demanded a third. "Give us what's ours now, or you're gonna regret it." The voices of the angry underworlders resounded through the crack they were forcing wider.

As Jas gasped with the effort of trying to hold back the furious men and women, Sayen got out of bed. She winced as she hobbled over.

"No," Jas and Carl said at once. But they were no match for the underworlders forcing their way in. Sooner or later, they would be pushed aside.

Favoring her good leg, Sayen stood between them and leant the strength of her enhanced body to their efforts. The cupboard slowly moved back and the door closed, shutting out the yells and shouts. As the door shut, Jas reached down into the bag of weapons she'd dropped when she'd rushed to stop the underworlders from getting in. She pulled out a blaster and went to stand grimly at the edge of the cupboard next to the wall.

Just let them try.

She didn't have to wait long. The underworlders must have gotten something they could use as a battering ram. A heavy weight struck the door, and the cupboard, Carl, and Sayen were thrown forward. A gap appeared, filled with triumphant underworlders. Their expressions quickly changed when Jas shoved a blaster in their faces.

"If you don't leave us alone," she said, "I'm going to barbecue the first head I see."

The gap was suddenly empty. She nodded at Carl, who pushed against the cupboard and closed the door.

"How long's it gonna take them to get some more guns?" he asked.

"Not long, I don't think," Jas said. "Not with their connections. But we've got a little more time. I wish I knew who took that invisibility spray."

"My bet's on our grumpy friend," Carl said.

"I think you're probably right. It looks like he was one of Erielle's right-hand men. I doubt she told many people about that spray."

"He's probably been maneuvering for a takeover for a while," Sayen said. "I'd love it if Erielle came back and put him in his place."

"We'd all love it if Erielle came back," Jas said. "And let's hope she does. But for now, we've only got ourselves and a little time until the underworlders gather enough firepower to force us out. We should take turns keeping watch tonight. I'll go first. You all try to get some sleep. We might have to leave tomorrow, whether we're ready or not."

"No, Jas," Carl said. "You sleep, and I'll take first watch. You didn't sleep all last night, and you've been up all day. I managed a nap this afternoon. Get some rest, and I'll watch the door."

He was right. She was exhausted, and that made her a liability in a fight. She spread some blankets on the floor and lay down. Carl took her place by the doorway, a blaster in his hand. Jas's eyes were only closed for a moment, however, before they snapped open and she sat bolt upright.

"What's wrong?" asked Sayen, who had made her way over to her bed.

"We've been forgetting something," Jas replied. "The most important thing. The minister."

"Krat. You're right," said Carl. "How long has she been in the basement by herself?"

"Sayen," Jas said. "It's awfully quiet out there. Can you hear anything?"

Sayen returned, limping, to the doorway. She put her ear against the wall. "They're right outside," she said quietly. Her eyes widened. "I can hear footsteps going downstairs. There's only one room down there. They're going to get the minister."

"Krat. Krat. Krat," exclaimed Jas. "We can't let them take her. Carl, open the door." Dipping her hand into the bag, she pulled out the first gun she touched. It was a small beamer, but anything would do. Carl was pushing their barricade out of the way. "Sayen, get something to protect yourself with. Carl, come with me, and bring that blaster."

"I'll come too," said Makey.

"Don't be stupid," Jas replied. "Stay here."

By the time Jas and Carl left the medical treatment room, the underworlders had all disappeared downstairs. Jas tiptoed after them, and Carl did the same. From the top of the stairs, Jas could see that the door to the basement room was open. She raced down, taking multiple steps at a time. She didn't know what they might do to the minister. They could have decided that keeping her was too much of a risk and were going to kill her.

She burst into the room, seemingly just in time. The large underworlder who wanted them to leave had a knife to the terrified woman's throat. At the sight of Jas he tensed and grabbed the minister, as if intending to block his body with hers. Jas fired before he could take another step. He slumped to the floor. The rest of the underworlders backed away.

"I've only stunned him," Jas said. "But that can soon change. Against the wall. All of you." The underworlders shuffled back, their eyes on her blaster. "Carl, cut her free. We'll take her upstairs with us."

Picking up the knife the fallen underworlder had dropped, Carl quickly sliced through the minister's bonds. The woman tried to rise to her feet, but either long sitting or simple fear had made her legs weak, and she staggered. Carl pulled her upright and put her arm over his shoulders. As he helped her to the door, Jas walked backward, keeping her aim fixed on the underworlders. Their would-be leader was already coming around. Jas was sorely tempted to put an end to his threat once and for all, but she couldn't bring herself to kill the man in cold blood. As well as the immorality of shooting him while he was defenseless, she also knew that her act would unite the underworlders against them. She hoped that people loyal to Erielle still existed among them, and though they might not be future friends, they might be allies.

No underworlders appeared in the doorway to the basement room as Jas, Carl, and their captive made their way up the stairs. They ran into the medical room, Carl still supporting the minister. The second they were safely inside, they replaced the barricade.

Her hair disheveled and her face a mask of shock, Bathsheba Dubois collapsed onto a chair and put her face in her hands.

"What happened?" Makey asked.

"I think our friend was going to kill her," Jas said grimly.

The minister's head lifted. "He said...he said if I didn't tell them everything I knew about what happened to confiscated mythranil, he would...he said he would cut my throat."

"Myth?" Jas asked. The underworlder's actions were beginning to make sense to her. Myth was an outrageously expensive drug. The man had to be an addict. If he were to take over as underworlder leader in the neighborhood, he would have the connections and resources to fund his habit. That was why he was in such a hurry to take Erielle's place.

4

It was a long night. Jas had insisted that Sayen rest and not keep watch. She slept head to toe with Makey in his bed. The minister took the other bed, but slept fitfully. When she did sleep, she snored and kept everyone awake.

Carl made Jas sleep again while he took the first watch. She curled up on the blankets on the floor. The underworlders' house was quiet. They seemed to have given up on dealing with them for the moment. He wondered if they were waiting on something—a new supply of weapons to arrive, for instance—or if they were arguing among themselves about what to do next. There had only been a few supporters down in the basement with the wannabe leader. He didn't seem a very likable bloke. He doubted that all of the others were behind him. There were probably quite a few who were holding out hope that Erielle would return. Though her leadership style was rough and ready, she'd seemed fair. She'd appeared to care about the people she led. He had a strong feeling the new guy only wanted to exploit them.

He watched Jas as she slept. The faint lines that time and a stressful job had worn into her face faded away, and she looked younger and more carefree, though he wasn't sure that she'd ever really been carefree. From the little she'd told him about her childhood, she'd led a lonely life. When they'd been watching for their Shadow target to leave the security headquarters, she'd told him something had happened to her years before in Antarctica that had made her never want to go back.

Sometimes, with the way she acted, Jas was a hard person to warm to. But Carl had found that, whatever she did that pushed him away, he couldn't help but be drawn back again each time. There was something different about her. Something he couldn't define in words, which connected with him deep inside. The longer he spent with her, the stronger the feeling grew.

He hoped that they would both make it out of whatever was coming, but if they didn't, he would be glad for the moments he'd spent with her.

After a few more hours, he yawned and rubbed his eyes. A pale, pre-dawn light was coming through the window. Carl had watched and listened for the underworlders all night, allowing Jas and the others to rest. He stood and stretched. His movement caused Jas to wake.

She sat up and saw that dawn wasn't far away. "What's the time?" she asked quietly. "Why didn't you wake me?"

"I was enjoying watching you sleep," he said.

"Right...That's a little bit creepy, Carl."

"You pull faces like my granny used to make when she was trying not to fart."

Jas opened her mouth in outrage. "No, I don't." She frowned. "Do I?"

Carl raised his eyebrows at her but didn't answer, as if he were trying to be kind.

"Oh, shut up. Of course I don't." She got out of bed. "Here, give me that blaster. You try to get some sleep. The underworlders might leave us alone for another hour or two." She came over to him and took his gun. "I don't really pull faces, right?"

He patted her on the shoulder. "Don't worry, Jas. It's kinda cute."

She narrowed her eyes at him as he went, smirking, to the blankets she'd just vacated. He lay down and turned on his side before allowing sleep to overwhelm him. Before he could sink into its depths, however, a massive thump against the door threw the cupboard to the floor. Medical devices, instruments, and other equipment spilled out. Jas stunned the first underworlder that burst into the room. He was unconscious before he fell onto his face, apparently breaking his nose, as blood flooded from beneath him.

Carl was already up and leaping to join her.

"The next one, I shoot to kill," shouted Jas. The underworlders took no notice. More were pouring into the room. Jas yelled as she was hit. Carl smelled her burnt flesh. The underworlders weren't pulling their punches. A man screamed as Jas's shot caught him square in the stomach. He stared in disbelief at the burning, gaping hole before his eyes rolled back and he toppled like a felled tree.

This made the rest pause, but only for a moment. Someone behind urged them on. The would-be leader, Carl guessed. Then he noticed the attacking underworlders' wild eyes and glistening skin. They were running on something. Their instigator had given them a drug to erode their judgment and get them to take part in this suicide mission.

As these thoughts sped through his mind, Carl was firing at the encroaching underworlders. He severed a man's leg at the knee. The sight of this caused another to turn and flee, despite the workings of the drug in his system. His action caused a body jam in the narrow doorway. The sound of screaming came from behind Carl. It sounded like the minister.

Jas's face was twisted with pain from the wound on her shoulder, but she fired off another shot, hitting a barrel-chested man who was managing to force his way through the struggling bodies. She got him in the neck and must have hit an artery because blood spurted out, pulsing with the man's heartbeats. He didn't seem to even notice. He continued to shove and shoulder the others aside until finally he was free, and he took an exultant step into the room. He lifted a weapon—new supplies had obviously arrived—and aimed at Carl.

In response, Carl squeezed his trigger, but he needn't have bothered. Before he could fire a shot, Jas scored a hit and the man fell upon the other she'd stunned. That one was now beginning to rise, but the weight of the falling, dying man smashed him to the floor and pinned him down.

Outside, a shout cut through the yells and cries of the attacking underworlders. They paused, and the noise quieted.

"I said, what the krat's going on?"

It was a man's voice: deep, confident, and commanding. Though it was unfamiliar to Carl, the underworlders clearly recognized who it belonged to. The effect was immediate. Those who had been trying to force their way in through the ones trying to get out ceased their efforts. The jam in the doorway disappeared as the attacking underworlders seemed almost to melt into thin air. Carl peered out into the hallway. There was no sign of the would-be leader, but the owner of the powerful voice stepped into view.

He was tall. Well over two meters. But he wasn't lanky like Carl. His height was matched in proportion by his girth, though he didn't seem to have an ounce of fat on him. The man's appearance was striking, and Carl took note of his coloring. His skin was a deep olive, and his thick, wavy hair was reddish-brown—a color that matched his eyes. The man was a Martian, like Jas.

In two strides of his well-muscled legs, he was in the room. His gaze roved over Makey and Sayen, who were sitting up in bed, then to the minister, who had drawn her covers up to her nose, and finally to Jas, Carl, and the one trapped and two dead underworlders. With the toe of his boot, he lifted the corpse off the underworlder pinned beneath it, and the bloody-faced man scrambled to his feet and was gone in the blink of an eye.

The newcomer put his hands on his hips. "Who the krat are you?"

5

Everyone in the room froze for a moment as they took in this new turn of events. Carl was first to break the ice. He stepped forward and held out his hand. "Carl Lingiari." The man took his hand and enveloped it in his own large, powerful grip. "Ozment. Just Ozment." He turned to Jas. The pain from her shoulder wound was etched on her face.

"You need something for that. Erielle can treat you. But where is she? What's going on here?"

"Erielle's missing," said Jas.

Ozment's eyes widened, and his hands fell from his hips. "What? No. For how long?"

"About thirty hours," Carl replied.

Raising a hand and running it through his hair, Ozment said, "Krat. Where did she go?"

"Don't you wanna ask your mates?" Carl asked. "You're one of her crew, right?"

"No. Not exactly. And from the way they took off when I arrived, like mice caught eating the cheese...if Erielle's not here...I'm guessing Durfy's behind this."

"Is he a big bloke?" asked Carl, and he went on to describe the underworlder.

"Yeah. I warned Erielle about him, but she obviously didn't listen to me. Too trusting." He turned to Jas, who was lifting the neck of her shirt, trying to peak underneath to her shoulder. "Let's get you seen to, then you can explain what's going on here."

Jas turned her attention to Ozment. "Yes, and you can explain who you are and what you're doing here."

A slight smile curved his lips. "Fair enough."

"Let me do it, Jas," Sayen said, easing herself out of bed. "I've been in enough doctors' offices and had enough treatments to be able to figure some of this out. I'll try to find a painkiller." She began pulling out drawers and riffling through their contents.

Ozment took a package from his back pocket and opened it. Inside the folded leather were some dried leaves. He picked out a few and handed them to Jas. "While you're waiting, chew on these. They'll take the edge off the pain." As Jas hesitated, he added, "It's kratom. It won't hurt you. People have been using it for thousands of years."

Jas took the leaves and put them in her mouth. As she began to chew, her nose wrinkled.

"Yeah, it's bitter. I'll make some kratom tea in a little while and sweeten it with honey to take away the taste."

Sayen made Jas sit down. She'd found a pair of scissors, and she used them to cut away the burned fabric, exposing red and blistered skin with a blackened patch at the edge of Jas's shoulder. Sayen winced and sucked air through her teeth. "Looks like the beam only grazed you. You were lucky. You could have lost your arm. I'll inject a local anesthetic that'll numb the wound for a while. Then I'll clean it up and put a sterile dressing on."

"Thanks," said Jas. "It's great that you can help now that Erielle isn't here. We can't risk any hospital visits with so many Shadows around."

"Shadows?" asked Ozment. "Looks like a lot's happened since my last delivery."

"I'll explain," Carl said.

But Jas interrupted, "No, don't." She turned to Ozment. "I'm sorry. I think you might have saved all our skins back there, but we don't know who you are. We can't trust everyone who walks in the door. We don't have that luxury."

Ozment shrugged. "That isn't unreasonable, I guess. How about I tell you who I am? Then you can have your turn."

"It doesn't matter who you are," said Jas. "This isn't a situation where we can trade secrets. I'm sorry. Thanks for your help."

Jas's words were followed by an awkward pause. Ozment shrugged again and went to Bathsheba's bed. She still had the covers drawn halfway up to her face as she stared at the man. "Do you mind if I sit here?" he asked her. Silently, she shook her head. Carl wondered why the woman didn't tell him who she was. He supposed she didn't want to give away her identity, especially since she'd had her life threatened twice in the last couple of days.

Bathsheba's bed creaked as Ozment sat down, flattening the edge of her mattress. Looks passed between Sayen, Jas, Makey, and Carl. It didn't look like the newcomer was going away for a while.

"This is what Erielle injected me with when she removed my tracker," Sayen said to Jas, holding up a bottle of clear liquid. "Are you okay with me using it on you?"

Her jaw muscles clenched, Jas nodded.

"How come the underworlders took off when you arrived?" Carl asked Ozment.

The Martian opened his pack of kratom and pinched a few leaves. He put them in his mouth and began to chew before he answered. "I guess they're a little scared of me. Either that or they don't want to lose their main supplier." He lifted a haunch as he returned the package to his back pocket. "I bring their kratom. Every month or so. Not so regular that the authorities get a handle on my delivery schedule."

"Erielle told us about it," Sayen said, holding a hypodermic syringe full of anesthetic poised over Jas's shoulder. "She said it's the main currency around here."

"Kratted stuff," Jas said between her teeth as Sayen slid the needle just beneath her skin. "I was constantly confiscating it and having it destroyed aboard ship. I don't know how the misborns used to smuggle it aboard."

"It's no more harmful than alcohol," said Ozment. "In a lot of ways it's less so."

"Yeah," Jas said. "I used to confiscate alcohol too."

Ozment smiled and moved his kratom cud from one side of his mouth to the other. "So you worked on starships?"

Jas frowned. "Krat."

The Martian laughed. "Don't worry. You don't have anything to fear from me, I swear. I just told you I'm a drug dealer. You could call the police right now, but I'm guessing you won't."

A pregnant silence stretched out. Carl felt an instinctive trust for the man, but he also knew that Jas was right. They shouldn't give away their identities and intentions to just anyone who walked in the door.

Ozment leaned back and stretched out his arms behind his back to support himself. "My story's pretty simple. I'm a farmer and kratom grower, down in the Everglades. Erielle's been my contact for a long time. I trade kratom in the city for items you can't get in the swamp."

"But you didn't always live in the Everglades, did you?" Carl asked. "You're a Martian."

"There's no denying it, as this woman will testify." He winked at Jas. "The original gene therapy that protects against radiation leaves an indelible mark on all that planet's inhabitants. But that was a long time ago. I've lived on Earth more than twenty years. I'd like to go back to Mars some day. Visit my folks. My old home. But I'll have to wait until the Government allows felons to space travel."

Intent as they all were on Ozment's life story, no one noticed the approaching footsteps. The underworld leader wannabe, the man Ozment called Durfy, appeared at the door. Ozment straightened up and fixed the man with a glare from under his brows. "I was wondering when you'd show your face. Been causing trouble again, I see."

"There's no trouble here," Durfy said. "Or if there is, I'm not the one causing it. I don't know what these folks have told you, but they roped Erielle into some risky business, and now it looks like she isn't coming back. I was just trying to make it clear to them that they've outstayed their welcome."

"You sure made it clear enough," Ozment replied. "But, whatever's happened to Erielle, if these people are here under her say so, that stands until we know for sure she's gone. She's no fool. You know that. If she trusted them, so should you. And you've got no authority to be evicting her guests anyway. You know the rules. Everyone gets to vote on a new leader. You can't just step up and take over, however much you might like the idea."

Durfy bristled a little at this accusation. "Who said I was

trying to take over? I was concerned for the others' safety with these strangers hanging around. Four people have gone missing due to them."

Carl gave a snort of derision and rubbed the scar on his wrist where the underworlders had cut out his credchip. "Listen, mate. The only one up to no good around here is you. You gave your friends something and riled them up to attack us. Until Erielle's back or we find her, we're sticking around, whether you like it or not. You got it?"

Durfy gave Carl a dirty look, but he left.

The tension in the room eased. Ozment's arrival had averted a crisis, but Carl didn't know how long they had before Durfy managed to rally enough support to evict them and assume Erielle's position.

6

———

A kind of normality returned to Erielle's household. Sark offered to cook them breakfast, and Ozment left to arrange the unloading of his kratom delivery. Despite the night's sleep Carl had kindly allowed her, Jas felt bone weary. The local anesthetic Sayen had injected was wearing off, and her wound ached with a pain that reached out from her shoulder, all the way down her arm, and to the back and front of her torso. She would have liked nothing more than to lie down again and sleep the rest of the day away, if she could ignore the pain. She'd been hit before, but this time seemed worse than the others. She hoped the wound wouldn't become infected.

Makey was still far from recovered, and Sayen was hobbling around with her sore butt. Carl was the only one left whole and healthy out of the four of them. Jas didn't have the luxury of slowing down or taking it easy. They seemed no farther forward with their plan of capturing a Shadow to take to the Transgalactic Council.

Bathsheba Dubois had finally relaxed enough to let go of her covers. She was resting her arms on them. As she caught Jas looking at her, she said, "What are you going to do with me? Are you going to let me go now? If you take me into the city and drop me somewhere, I'll walk away. I won't tell anyone about you, or about this place. I promise."

Jas shook her head. "You know we can't trust you. And, anyway, kidnapping you is the least of our worries. We're trying to do something more important than you, or me. We're trying to save the Earth from invasion."

"Yes, yes, I know. The Shadows. But the Government nearly has the situation under control. There's no need for you to do anything. In another few months, we'll have rooted out the last of them, and—"

"No, you won't," exclaimed Jas. "You don't have any idea how bad the situation is. We have to do something. Now. I don't care about quarantine and trade embargos. That's all about money. I'm talking about lives. Human beings who are right now being murdered and replaced by aliens. If you ministers won't put a stop to it, we will."

"All right, all right," Bathsheba said, raising her hands. "I hear what you're saying, and you've convinced me. If you set me free, I promise I'll take your message back to the Global Government. I'll insist they hold an inquiry about the true state of affairs regarding the Shadow invasion of Earth."

For a moment, Jas almost couldn't believe her ears. *An inquiry?* She couldn't believe that someone who was responsible for the safety of every human being on the planet could be so out of touch and so blind to the reality of what was happening. Jas did the only thing she could in response to the minister's ridiculous words. She laughed. Loudly, uproariously, she laughed until her stomach ached.

When she could laugh no more, she wiped her eyes. Bathsheba was looking at her and the others—who had heard the conversation and had the same reaction as Jas—as if they were mad. Then she began to sob. Her face in her hands, between muffled sniffs, she said, "Please, please let me go. I don't know what's so funny about what I said, but you have to let me go. That man...that man was going to kill me, and it's only a matter of time before he returns to finish me off."

Jas felt a twinge of guilt. It was true. Bathsheba had come perilously close to losing her life only a few hours ago. Prior to that she'd been chased, captured, gagged, tied, put in the trunk of a car, driven to an unknown destination, and finally been held captive against her will among a group of strangers who seemed intent on doing her harm.

But though she felt a little sorry for Bathsheba, she definitely didn't want to let her go just yet. There was still a remote chance that she was a Shadow. After all, Sayen had been convinced that the Shadow who'd had her kidnapped had been a nice, older man.

"What if I tell you how you can test whether I'm a Shadow?" Bathsheba asked. "Would you let me go then, if I can prove to you that I'm not?"

This caught everyone's attention.

"How would you do that?" asked Sayen.

"A year or so ago," Bathsheba said, "we received a shipment of scanners from the Transgalactic Council. Shadows had appeared and begun to spread across the galaxy, and they wanted us to protect Earth by scanning everyone who arrived from other planets. We had to invent a whole load of other tests to put Shadows off the scent of the new technology, but it's only the scanner that works."

"We know that," said Sayen. "I found out about it just before the Shadow working in your office arranged my capture."

"You're proposing that we scan you?" Carl asked the minister.

"Yes, exactly."

"And how are we going to do that?" asked Jas.

"The scanners have a finite life. We have to replace them every three months. A new shipment is due from the Council next week."

"And...?" Jas asked.

"Well, I never thought I'd be saying this, but I can give you the information to help you steal one. If you manage it, however, you have to test me. When you know for sure that I'm not a Shadow, you have to let me go. Is it a deal?"

A Shadow scanner? It was exactly what they needed. Otherwise, they were operating by guesswork. They would have only one chance to show the Transgalactic Council that there were Shadows on Earth. They had to get it right and be sure they had a real Shadow to prove what they were saying.

"What do you think, guys?" she asked Carl, Sayen, and Makey.

"How well-protected is the shipment?" Sayen asked.

"That's the advantage of my suggestion," Bathsheba replied. "It isn't that well-protected. Research has shown that the more attention you draw to something with a heavy deployment of security, the greater the chances are of an attack. The scanners are arriving in a shipment of regular imports from deep space. Only I and one other trusted person know the carrier, and the day, time, and place of the arrival."

"When is it?" asked Jas.

"In six days."

"I don't know," Jas said. "We aren't in much of a state to be breaking into a spaceport."

"I'll be fine in a couple of days," Makey said.

"I'm up for it," said Carl.

Sayen said, "I'll be better soon too. My skin's completely healed. It's just the muscles underneath that are still a little sore. But I don't know that I agree with this idea. It'd feel like we're abandoning Erielle. After all she did for us, we should try to find her. I keep thinking that she's out there somewhere, hurt but unable to get any help. We should at least return to the Security HQ and scout around a little. Something bad has happened to her, or she'd be back by now for sure. As long as there's a chance she's alive, we shouldn't give up on her."

"You're right," Jas said. "We owe her, and if it weren't for the problems with these kratted underworlders, I would have gone out looking for her before now. Maybe we can do both. If this shipment of Shadow scanners isn't due until next week, we have plenty of time to look for Erielle."

"And," Carl said, "we don't have to decide right away if we're going after the scanners. Maybe something else'll turn up."

Ozment appeared, and the discussion immediately dried up. The Martian rubbed his hands together and said with a smirk, "My entrance hasn't had that effect since I had too much kratom and walked naked into a local government planning meeting."

7

———

As soon as he heard about their plan to try to find Erielle, Ozment wanted in on it. At first, Jas wouldn't accept his help, but Sayen had pointed out that Jas's and Carl's faces were already known to the Shadows at Security HQ from their first kidnapping attempt. It wouldn't be long before they were noticed and apprehended. Now that the invisibility spray had gone missing, they couldn't get too close to the building, but Ozment was someone Erielle would recognize as a friend, and he certainly stood out, making him easy for her to see.

Finally, Jas relented. "You're still not one hundred percent, so I don't think you should come," she said to Sayen, "but I'm not comfortable with leaving you, Makey, and the minister here unprotected. Durfy and his lackies might have backed off for the moment, but who's to say they won't change their minds, especially if Ozment's out of the picture for the day?"

"I can deal with them," Sayen said. "Durfy knows what I'm capable of. He was there when I broke into the medical center to steal the blood for Makey, and he's no fool."

"No, he isn't," Jas replied. "Which is why he drugged up a bunch of his followers and used them as cannon fodder before he showed his face in here. Two underworlders died. That's two too many. I don't want any more deaths. I hope you don't mind me saying, Sayen, but you don't exactly look intimidating. It wouldn't take much for Durfy to persuade the underworlders to risk an attack against a sick kid, a soft politician, and a little woman."

Sayen bit her lip. "I guess you're right. I don't want to hurt anyone."

"Then I'll go by myself," Ozment said. "Just give me directions."

"No," said Makey. "At least two of you have to go. You'll be safer in pairs."

"True," Jas said. "I'm glad to see you're getting a little better understanding of security, Makey. Okay. Ozment and I will go. As a pair of Martians wandering around, we'll be noticed, but people will think we're tourists. Just a couple out doing a little sight-seeing. Carl, you can stay here as an extra deterrent to the underworlders."

"But how're you going to get there without me?" Carl asked. "You can't park that limo anywhere. It'll stick out like a sore thumb. And that old car we used for the first kidnapping is a self-driver. Can you drive, Jas?"

"I can drive," Ozment said. "We have plenty of self-drivers down in the Everglades."

Carl looked as though he still didn't agree, but he said nothing.

Life at Erielle's place had become seriously disorganized in her absence. No one seemed to know who they should talk to about borrowing the car they needed to get to the Security HQ. Some underworlders seemed to believe that Durfy was in charge, and that they were no longer welcome there; others appeared frightened to speak to them. A few were simply apathetic, lying semi-conscious in the communal bedrooms, heavily drugged up.

Ozment's expression became graver as he and Jas continued their inquiries. "The sooner we find Erielle and bring her back here, the better," he said after they had interrupted two men paying what had seemed to be too much unwanted attention to a young woman. "Back home, there's plenty to do on the farm. It keeps people focused. Living in the city seems to bring out the worst in people. They need someone strong, with a clear purpose. Someone who leads by example. Erielle's is one of the best underworld neighborhoods. I hate to think what's going to happen if she's gone."

Finally, they happened upon Sark in the kitchen. Of all the house's inhabitants, she appeared to be the only one who had continued as normal, faithfully cooking three meals a day for the entire household. They found her instructing three small boys on how to peel potatoes. She was leaning over them as they gazed in dismay at the large pile at their feet. When Jas and Ozment appeared, she straightened up, and her usually sharp face broke into a smile.

"Good to see you again, Ozment. Thanks for bringing our supplies. I've been a little busy with my apprentices, or I would have come and found you."

"It's good to see you too, Sark. I hope you haven't been too disturbed by the commotion going on around here."

She waved dismissively. "Oh, I don't ever get caught up

in all that nonsense. People come, people go. Sometimes they fight a little. No one bothers Sark if they want their supper."

"I'm glad to hear it," Ozment said. "And a delicious supper it is too, every time."

Sark smiled in a way that said she knew he was buttering her up, but she didn't mind. "So, what can I do for you?"

"We were wondering if you knew how we could borrow a vehicle to use on an errand we'd like to run."

"I sure do." Her expression clouded. "Are you going to look for Erielle? I heard she still isn't back."

"That's right. We are."

"Then wait here a minute, and I'll go and arrange it right away. I was hoping someone would do something. I couldn't bear it if anything's happened to that sweet woman."

While Sark was gone, a couple of the small boys tried to sneak away, but Ozment clapped his large hands on their boney shoulders and turned them around. They slunk back onto their stools and picked up their potato peelers and a potato each. They looked in puzzlement from the peelers to the potatoes, as if trying to figure out how the two fit together. The third boy was busy stabbing his potato with the pointed end of his peeler.

Sark returned and told them a car with a full battery would be out in the street for them in a moment. They thanked her. As they went outside, Jas said, "Those poor boys. That looked like a dirty, boring chore Sark had set up for them."

"You're thinking, wouldn't it be easier to put the potatoes in an electric peeler? Or better yet, buy them ready-prepared? Or even better, just buy the whole meal and heat it up?"

"I guess so," Jas said as she got into the car on the passenger side.

Ozment sat in the driver's seat. "Well, you know, we do the same thing down in the Everglades. We teach the kids how to prepare and cook food. We also teach them how to clean, do simple first aid, how to build shelters, hunt, and grow their own vegetables, fruit, grains, and beans. It might seem like a waste of time to you digifreaks, but you never know, one day humans might need all the old skills again just to survive."

He started the car, and they set off. He continued, "But it's more than that. We teach our kids these things not only so they know how to look after themselves without help from technology, but also so that they learn patience, attention to detail, concentration, how to work with others...lots of things. It isn't all about survival skills. I know we must seem like backward savages, but it's a good life we lead. It's an honest and happy one."

Jas hesitated to reply, but she couldn't square Ozment's statements with what she'd seen of the underworlders so far. "I don't know. Do you really think the underworlders hereabouts are happy? They don't seem to be leading very honest lives. "

"It's harder in the city. There's a lot of crime and a lot of prejudice against naturals. Sometimes they have to do unsavory things to survive. They would be better off in the country. I've often tried to persuade Erielle to come down and live with us, but her followers are used to city life. They won't leave, and she won't leave them."

They were exiting the underworld neighborhood and heading downtown to the business and government district.

Jas tried to imagine where Erielle might have gone if she were injured. She regretted not arranging a place where they could meet in such an eventuality. They'd only spoken in terms of the success or failure of the plan.

Ozment broke into her musings. "Where are you from on Mars?"

"Valles Marineris Five."

"Oh, krat. I'm sorry." He glanced at her. "But, you're...?"

"I was a baby when it happened."

"I see. I didn't think there were any survivors."

"I was the only one. My parents got me into a survival capsule just in time, but it was too late for them. The colony records were destroyed, so I don't know who they were. When I was twelve, the authorities shipped me to Earth to finish my education." She preferred to deal with the inevitable questions all at once. It got the subject out of the way.

Ozment considered a moment, then asked, "Did you know...you might be one of us?"

Jas turned to him. "What do you mean?"

"There were Green Earthers at Valles Marineris Five."

Jas slumped back. *Green Earthers, like the people on Dawn?* "How come? Surely Green Earthers wouldn't have wanted to undergo the anti-radiation gene therapy?"

"For the sake of forging a new life on a new, unspoilt planet, some of them were prepared to bend their morals a little. And, after all, it's just the once. As you know, the effect gets passed on, even to children naturally conceived, so there's no need for any further modding or unnatural alterations. All of us get to be this beautiful color." He gave her a wink.

The idea that Jas's parents might have been Green Earthers had never occurred to her. She'd always thought of them as ordinary colonists—adventurers, maybe, excited at the idea of life on a colony planet, or trying to escape poverty, or running away from some kind of trouble. She'd never thought that her mother and father might have been underworlders.

8

———

Jas directed Ozment to park in the alley where she and the others had stopped before their first attempt to kidnap Shadow Bernie.

"Where should we start looking?" he asked.

"The HQ is a couple of streets away, but I can't go near that place. The Shadows there know me. Out here should be safe enough for a little while. How about you go and check out all around the building? If she's there, she'll see you, and maybe she can attract your attention."

"But you said she went inside? If she's hurt, wouldn't she be there?"

"The only reason she got in there was because she was covered in invisibility spray. If you try to go in without ID, they'll arrest you. We have to hope that she managed to make it outside." The pit of Jas's stomach ached. "It's been two nights. I can't believe her supposedly loyal followers haven't tried to do something to find her."

"I think Durfy's behind that. There aren't many who'll go against him. But we're trying to do something now at least. Tell me where to go."

Jas explained how to get to the Security HQ. When Ozment left, she got out of the car and walked up and down the alley. She'd had a crazy hope that Erielle might have made her way there and was waiting for someone to come, but of course Erielle hadn't known they'd stopped in that spot.

She went to the end of the alley and looked out into the bustling street. Cabs and private cars buzzed by. Occasionally, a single-seater, low-slung autobike flashed through the traffic, most likely speeding, but few paid attention to speed limits. Computer-controlled cars meant that serious accidents were a thing of the past. Jas mused that Carl would probably love to ride an autobike.

There were few pedestrians. In the business districts, people went from their cars into the offices and back again. There was little reason to wander the streets. If Erielle was somewhere nearby, that fact would work in her favor. Few pedestrians meant few people likely to stumble across an invisible, injured woman.

Of course, the most likely reason for Erielle's absence was that she'd been killed or captured by Shadows. Jas hoped that if that was the case, that it was the former rather than the latter. She didn't want to face the problem of a Shadow Erielle turning up.

Standing in the street without any obvious purpose, Jas was attracting stares, so she returned to the car. After another twenty-five minutes, Ozment also came back. He'd found no sign of the missing underworld leader.

"That place is crawling with security agents, on foot and driving," he said. "People in suits and uniformed guards are patrolling the area. I had a look around, but there was no sign of any blood or anything that might lead us to Erielle. I hung about as long as I could. If Erielle was conscious, she would have seen me. I listened out in case she called me, but I didn't hear anything."

"Krat. I guess it was too much to hope for. Let's walk the route she would have taken if she were trying to get home. Maybe we'll find her on the way."

They set off. Jas put her arm through Ozment's but grimaced and went to his other side. Her shoulder wound was still painful. She linked arms with him again, so that they looked like a couple out for a stroll. The man's arm was firmly muscled. Jas imagined he must have a lot a physical labor in his work growing kratom. As they walked, they stopped at any likely spot where Erielle might be—in alleys, behind dumpsters, in disused doorways. They softly called her name, and surreptitiously ran their feet along the ground, hoping to meet an invisible obstruction.

"You know," Ozment said, "we could always break into the headquarters. If they caught her, they might still be holding her there."

"I'd like to think so," Jas replied, "but I doubt it. When they captured Sayen, they took her away to a trap immediately."

"A trap?"

Jas had forgotten Ozment still didn't know about the Shadows or the reason why Erielle had gone with them to capture someone from the Security HQ. She sighed. "Okay. I'll explain. But, please, you can't tell anyone. The reason why will become clear."

"If it might help Erielle, I can keep a secret."

"I'm sorry, but, honestly, I think Erielle's beyond our help. Do you still promise to keep this to yourself?"

"I do."

Jas looked into the man's reddish-brown eyes. As had lately become her habit, she searched for signs that he might be a Shadow. She saw none, and she had no bad feelings about him, but that didn't stop her from worrying that she might be mistaken. She wondered if she would ever lose that feeling about every new person she met.

She sighed again. "Let's go back to the car and drive through the area we've covered. Then we can park again and explore farther from there. When we've checked everywhere Erielle might be, I'll explain. I don't want to delay our search for her. We've delayed long enough."

They looked for the missing woman for the next few hours, but Erielle was nowhere to be found.

After they'd covered all the ground they could, they parked. Jas explained to Ozment about the Shadows and briefly went over what had happened since they'd first encountered them at K. 67092d.

"So, there's really no way to tell these Shadows apart from their victims?" Ozment asked when she'd finished.

"It depends. If you see one soon after they've made the switch, there's something odd about them. They look kind of empty, like there's nothing behind their eyes. And they lose concentration easily. We think they communicate telepathically and that sometimes they're having a conversation in their heads. But after a while, when they're used to their new bodies, no, you can't really tell. Not until one of them attacks you, of course.

"And the funny thing is, the closer you are, or the more friendly you feel toward one of them, the harder it is to notice they aren't who you think they are." She swallowed. "I was affectionate with a man on Dawn, and I didn't realize he'd been swapped with a Shadow. I just thought he was upset at me about something. He nearly got me into one of their traps. I ended up having to kill him."

"His Shadow, you mean."

"Yes, his Shadow. Of course."

Ozment was quiet for a moment. He looked out the car window. They'd stopped at the edge of the underworlder territory, and they were surrounded by dilapidated, abandoned, derelict buildings.

"If those misborns have captured Erielle," he said quietly, "we have to get her back."

"I want to too. But she probably isn't at the headquarters anymore. Anyway, I wouldn't even know how to get inside. I know you said we could break in, but that's the Global Government Security building for krat's sake. It isn't like you can pop a lock on a window and sneak inside."

"No. When I said break in," Ozment said, "I didn't mean like a burglar. I meant *break* in." He started the car. "I'll show you what I mean."

He drove the short distance back to Erielle's place, but he passed by the final turn and instead entered the next road, which was wider. A huge truck was parked at the other end of Erielle's alley.

"That's yours?" Jas asked.

"How else do you think I make my deliveries?"

"That's a monster."

He smiled. "Wait till you see inside."

They got out of their vehicle and went to the truck's cab. Ozment unlocked it, and Jas climbed in. The interior had a sweet, slightly rotten odor, which she assumed was the smell of kratom. The wide seats were covered in cracked, very soft material that also exuded an unusual smell. It took her a moment to realize what the material was.

"This is leather, isn't it?" she asked.

"Yeah. The truck's pretty old, but she's a good one, and we've made some modifications." Ozment looked up the street and checked the surround-view screens on the dashboard. The road was empty. He turned and opened an almost invisible, square door behind the seats. Jas saw a sloping tunnel with indentations for hands and feet, leading up into darkness.

"We created a false roof. Up there's a toy to keep the Shadows busy while we try to find Erielle."

"I admit I'm impressed, but why would you need heavy weaponry? That seems a little excessive, even for a kratom grower."

"When you live on the fringes of modern society, Jas, you need all the protection you can get."

"Okay, Ozment, but I don't see how a mortar or whatever it is that's up there will get us inside the HQ. It'll take a lot to get through their defenses."

"Okay, check this out." He thumbed a button, and the cab juddered as a metal wall rose to cover the windscreen. As darkness fell inside, the dashboard lit up with an electronic display that included a screen showing images from cameras on the outside. "That's reinforced, laser-proof steel. With that in front, and the power of this truck's engines, we could punch right through a solid wall."

9

———

When Jas and Ozment returned to Erielle's place, all hell had broken loose. Durfy had persuaded the other underworlders to launch another attack. This time, Jas got to see him at work from another perspective. He was standing on the stairs, watching as the drugged-up men and women tried to force their way into the medical center.

They'd arrived not a moment too soon, for the resistance inside the room had clearly collapsed, and the underworlders were streaming in. Ozment shouted at them as he had before, but he had less of an effect, maybe because his delivery was unloaded and safely in their possession. A shriek came from inside the room.

There was only one way to stop them, Jas realized. Instead of targeting the underworlders, she ran straight to Durfy. His gloating expression vanished when he saw her. He fumbled for something inside his jacket, but Jas had a weapon pressed against his temple before he could reach it.

"Call them off," she barked. "Now, or so help me, I'll—"

"Okay, okay," Durfy muttered.

Jas stuck a hand into his jacket and pulled out a blaster, which she tossed to Ozment. She forced Durfy down the stairs and into the medical center. The room was in chaos. Several bodies lay on the floor. Three underworlders were grappling with Sayen, and another was in a fistfight with Carl, who was trying to protect Makey. The remaining underworlders were dragging the minister from her bed. She was clinging to the headboard with her fingertips, but as Jas went in, they ripped her away and lifted her onto their shoulders.

The minister shrieked for a second time. Ozment followed them in and set upon the underworlders who were fighting with Sayen.

"Stop them, now," Jas shouted at Durfy.

"Okay, everyone, that's enough," the man said half-heartedly.

Jas ground the point of her weapon into his skull.

"That's enough," he repeated, louder. When the under-worlders still didn't respond, he said, "A new run for everyone who stops now."

That message got through, and the antagonists stopped fighting. The ones holding the minister dropped her onto the bed. Sayen took a moment too long to understand what was happening, and she thrust her elbow into the side of a man's head, sending him spinning to the floor. As she did so, she became aware that the fight was over. "Ooops, sorry."

"What about her?" asked an underworlder, indicating the minister. "You said she could get us some myth."

"Looks like I was wrong," Durfy replied.

"You're only saying that 'cos she'll kill you if you don't," said the underworlder, looking at Jas, who was maintaining her position with her gun pressed against Durfy's head.

"Come on, guys," said Ozment, his hands on his hips.

"Take a look at yourselves. What are you doing? These people are Erielle's guests. What kind of hospitality is this? Is this what underworlders stand for? Fighting women half your size?" He eyed Sayen, who was surrounded by three unconscious men. "Dragging old ladies from their beds?" The minister's eyes flashed, but she said nothing. "Is this what Erielle taught you? Is this how she'd like you to behave?"

"They're digifreaks. They don't deserve our respect," said an underworlder.

Ozment sighed and shook his head. "This is what comes of living out of touch with nature. *All* living things deserve your respect, especially other human beings. Sometimes we have to lie, and steal, and cheat. Sometimes we even have to kill. But we don't do it unless we have to. And we certainly don't do it for the sake of a run. What's wrong with you people? What nonsense has this man been whispering in your ears?"

"Oh, quit with the lecture," said another underworlder. "You come up from the country, thinking you can tell us what to do and how to live our lives. You don't live on the street. You don't know anything."

"Hey," Jas said. "I'm sick and tired of living here anyway. You don't want us here, so we'll leave. Just let us go in peace, okay? We'll be out of your way by this evening."

"You sure, Jas?" Carl asked.

"Yes. Are you well enough to move, Makey?"

"Yes, I am. I've been up and walking around today."

"Great."

"You're right," Sayen said. "It's time for us to go. But, in case you were wondering, she comes with us." She pointed at Bathsheba.

"No," Durfy said. "I'm not agreeing to that. She stays."

"Yeah, she can tell us where the myth is," said an underworlder.

"No, I can't," Bathsheba said shrilly. "I have no idea where it's kept. I can't help you with that. But when the police catch you, I do have the authority to uphold the death penalty if I feel you have threatened global security, which you can be assured I do."

"*If* the police catch us," said the underworlder. "Not seen a cop around here in the last five years. Anyone else?"

Another underworlder puffed air between relaxed lips. "I don't know. Probably not worth the risk. I heard that myth isn't all it's hyped up to be anyway."

"Look," said Ozment, "you let them walk out of here free —all of them—and I promise I won't hold a grudge. Delivery as normal next month. You don't want to lose your kratom, do you? Or the food I bring you? Come on, guys, see sense."

"Okay, let them go," said the second underworlder who had spoken. The first began to protest, but the others drowned him out with calls of agreement.

Durfy was scowling. "You've got an hour," he said between his teeth before stalking out of the room. The rest of the underworlders left with him, except the ones who were unconscious or dead.

"We're going to Erielle's safe house?" Sayen asked Jas.

"It seems for the best, don't you think? Do you still have the map?"

"I do. I take it you didn't find Erielle?"

"No, we didn't. I'm sorry."

Sayen looked down. "I guess it's better than finding her body."

Jas put a hand on her shoulder. "There's still hope.

Ozment here has an idea for storming the security HQ and rescuing her, if she's there."

"Storming that building?" Sayen snorted and shook her head. "No chance."

"You haven't seen his truck."

IT TOOK them less than an hour to pack up what little stuff they had. A lot of Erielle's medical supplies and equipment had been trashed in the fight, but Sayen picked through them and gathered up what she could that she thought might be useful. Makey still required regular dressing changes and antiseptic sprays, she explained. Sayen seemed to be taking along a lot more than that, Jas thought, but she didn't object. With Erielle gone, the remaining under-worlders seemed to be descending into a state where medical treatment would be low on their agenda.

They asked Sark if she wanted to come with them, but the woman said no. There were many young and innocent mouths to feed, and she wouldn't ever begrudge a meal to the worst of them. They were all human beings, after all. Ozment told her she was a person after his own heart, and that he hoped things were better when he returned in about a month.

They drove to the safe house in his truck. The cab was large enough for them all to squeeze in. Carl was so impressed with the vehicle he could barely speak. It wasn't far to their new place, but it was difficult to get there through the streets of the old neighborhood. Ozment had to drive out onto wider roads, then approach the house from a different direction.

Eventually, he stopped outside. It was a small building,

dwarfed by newer, but still very old apartment blocks on either side. The yard was overgrown, and it looked like no one had set foot on it in ages. The gate was ajar, and the windows were blank and dark. It was late dusk, and no lights shone from inside, which Jas was glad of. Everything indicated the house was unoccupied. She hoped none of Durfy's followers would find them there and try to force them out, for a few days at least.

She pushed at the gate, but it was stuck and wouldn't open any wider. She tried again. The hinge gave a moan. It was no use; the gate would only open wide enough for her to squeeze through. They would have to lift their belongings over.

As she stepped through, her foot caught on something, and she fell. Astonished, she looked back at whatever had tripped her. There was nothing there. It had been something large, soft—and invisible.

10

———

"What's wrong, Jas?" asked Sayen as she saw the woman's expression. They were on their way into the safe house, and she was holding a bundle of clothes they'd brought with them from Erielle's place. She gazed in wonder as she saw Jas drop down and begin manhandling something Sayen couldn't see. *Something she couldn't see.*

The clothes fell from her grasp, and for a moment she was frozen. Then she was at Jas's side, and she too could feel the warm, soft, invisible body beneath her hands. "Erielle," she gasped.

Jas had a handful of grass, and she was rubbing it on the prone figure. Bits and pieces of Erielle began to appear as she scrubbed off the invisibility spray. Her clothes, a part of an arm.

"Wait," said Sayen. She had figured out how the underworld leader was lying. She pushed her onto her back and pressed an ear between her breasts. "Be quiet," she hissed, as exclamations of realization came from Makey and Carl. The street had no traffic, but it still took several long seconds before Sayen heard a heartbeat. It was slow and faint, but it was there.

"Get the door open, Jas," said Ozment.

Sayen found Erielle being pulled from her grasp as the large man scooped her up in his arms. She followed him into the dark house and the first room they saw. Inside was a dusty, old sofa. He laid Erielle down on it. Someone found the light switch. Someone else was asking for soap and water. All Sayen could do was hold Erielle's invisible wrist and feel for the thready pulse. Then she heard the underworlder murmur.

"Wait, she's saying something," Sayen said to Jas, who was cleaning the spray from Erielle's face. She leaned close. Only Erielle's right cheekbone, ear, and eye were visible. Her skin was translucent and drawn tightly over her cheekbones. Her eye was sunken in its socket. Sayen bent down to her mouth.

Erielle was speaking so softly, she could barely make out what the woman was saying. "Oh-seven-three...four-seven...two..."

"Can you understand?" Jas asked.

Sayen nodded. "Wait a minute." She listened some more, and Erielle repeated herself twice. "Okay, Erielle, I've got it now," she said, but the woman didn't seem to hear her because she continued to repeat the numbers.

"What's she saying?" asked Ozment.

"I don't know. It's a set of ten numbers. Could it be a key lock? Or a code? Do underworlders use encryption codes?"

"Not that I've ever heard of," said Ozment. "Ten numbers? What if it's just a phone number?"

"A phone number? Of course. It might be just that. Could you call it for us?"

"I've got an interface in the cab of the truck. It's untraceable. Come with me."

Sayen followed the Martian to his vehicle and climbed inside. She spoke the number into the interface, and a call went through, but it was a long time before the callee picked up. A middle-aged man's face wearing a suspicious expression appeared on the screen.

"Hello? Who is this?"

"Hi," Sayen said, "you don't know me, but please don't hang up."

"Why can't I see your face? If you're selling—"

"I'm not selling anything. I got your number from someone who's in need of help. She's saying this number over and over again. I think she wants me to call you."

The man's expression changed from suspicion to annoyance. "I'm sorry, I think maybe you have a wrong number. Anyone I know who's in need of help would go to the..." He paused, and a look of recognition began to dawn on his face. "Who is this person?"

"Her name's Erielle, and she's very, very badly hurt."

"Erielle," breathed the man. "After all this time. Where are you calling from? I'll be right there."

Ozment gave the man the address. He frowned as he took it and seemed to momentarily reconsider his decision, but before he hung up, he said he would be there in twenty minutes.

When they got back inside, Jas had cleaned all the invisibility spray from Erielle, and at the sight of her, Sayen nearly collapsed. A deep laser wound ran across both her thighs, halfway to her knees. The muscle was visible, and Sayen thought she could even see bone. Her arms were also a mess. Unable to walk, Erielle must have dragged herself on her arms all the way from the Security

HQ. She bore dark red scabs from her elbows to her wrists.

Jas was dripping water into her mouth, but some was running out unswallowed, as Erielle continued to mouth the phone number over and over again.

"She made it all this way," said Sayen. "Why didn't she come back to us?"

"I guess she couldn't make it any farther," Jas said. "Not even a few more streets. She must have seen the safe house, dragged herself inside, and collapsed."

"How long has she been lying there?" Sayen asked. "Oh why didn't we come here earlier? If only we'd left last night."

"We're here now. We've found her, and she's safe. Did someone answer your call?"

"Yes. I think it was an old friend from when she was a doctor. He said he's coming over."

"She used to be a doctor?" Jas asked. "I never knew, but it makes sense."

Sayen knelt by the sofa and looked more closely at Erielle's thighs. They were a mess, and at close range, Sayen detected a putrid, rotting odor. The wounds were going bad. Sayen prayed that she was right in guessing that the man she'd called was a surgeon, and that—somehow—he could save Erielle's legs.

Then it hit her. "What are we doing?" she said. "This is crazy. Erielle could die. Nothing's worth that. I'm going to call an ambulance." She went to return to Ozment's truck, but she found her way barred by the man's large frame.

"No," he said. "Erielle wouldn't want it."

"You don't know that," said Sayen. "I'm pretty sure she'd want to live." She tried to sidestep Ozment, but he moved to block her again.

"I do know that," he said gently. "I've known her a long

time. She *would* rather die than be a part of a system that's caused so much pain and suffering in our world."

"You mean the medical system? That's saved so many lives and cured so many people?" Sayen asked shrilly. "Erielle told me what she found out, but this is different. This is life or death."

"This isn't the time for a debate. I can see how deeply you care about her. We have to respect her wishes."

Sayen clenched her fists and tried to hold back the hot tears that sprang unwanted to her eyes. Deep down, she knew Ozment was right. In the short time she'd known Erielle, she'd made her disgust for modern health services and their obsession with human perfection very clear. But Sayen felt so helpless. She couldn't bear to stand by and watch Erielle pass away.

There was a quiet knock at the front door. Ozment moved aside, and Sayen ran to open it. The man she'd called was waiting, a black case in his hand. He glanced from side to side before entering.

The sight of Erielle made him pause a moment, as if he didn't recognize her at first. He shook his head and went to her side. "My dear friend, whatever's happened to you?" he asked. Opening his case, he said without looking around, "I need one person to assist me. The rest of you, out."

"I'll help," blurted Sayen, and she sprang to the man's side.

11

———

Three days had passed, and they had three days still to go before the shipment of Shadow scanners from the Transgalactic Council arrived. They'd found dried food stored in the safe house to keep them going. Jas was in the back yard. Once, a lawn must have grown there, but now the area was a mess of weeds and trash that had blown in from the street. The sun was hot and the air was humid. She sat alone on an old swing seat on the porch, leaning against the decayed wooden slats, which were coated in ancient, flaking paint.

The mysterious man Sayen had called had just delivered the news that, after several dicey moments, it looked like Erielle would live. The man never gave his name, and whenever he turned up, he spent most his time with his patient. They had turned the living room into a bedroom as the man had advised, saying that he didn't want to risk even moving Erielle to another room.

The underworld leader's wounds were free of infection at last and on the mend, and she was able to eat and drink normally. He'd said she needed surgery to walk again, but so far she'd refused all mention of such treatment.

Try as she might, Jas couldn't understand why anyone in their right mind would rather be paraplegic than undergo restorative surgery. But that was Erielle's choice, she decided, and ceased worrying about it. She had to plan their next course of action, but the gentle rocking of the seat and the heat of the day were sending her into a doze.

They no longer had to concern themselves with finding Erielle, which meant they no longer had to go through with Ozment's plan of storming the security HQ. They could focus instead on stealing one of the Shadow scanners. But the spaceport where the scanners were arriving was a state away, and they had to make their attempt when it was dark. They would have to spend a night on the road on their way there, Jas calculated. She needed time to scope out the site in daylight and plan the best method for breaking in and getting out alive.

In her bedroom were all the weapons that she and Carl had taken from Erielle's stash, and Ozment had some serious artillery in his truck, so firepower wouldn't be too much of a problem. It was really that there were so few of them that made the project risky. She didn't want anyone to get hurt. If only she had ten or fifteen deep space defense units, she would feel much more confident.

The back door opened with a squeak of rusty hinges, and Makey came out. He no longer wore a dressing over the wound on his neck. It was healing nicely, and a shiny, pink scar was forming. Jas got the impression that the kid was rather proud of it.

"Hey, Jas," he said. "Did you hear the news? Erielle's going to be okay."

"Yeah, I heard. It's great news."

Makey sat down next to her, pushing the swing backward. "So what are we going to do now? Are we going to break into a spaceport and steal some scanners?"

"Hmmm...so you overheard the minister? Well, I was just thinking about that, but I'm not sure what you mean by *we*."

"Awww, come on. You have to let me come too."

"I *have* to? Do I?"

Makey groaned. He jumped to his feet, performed a mock salute and said, "Permission to come too, ma'am."

Jas laughed. "Sit down. I don't know. I haven't decided yet, to be honest. Someone has to stay with Erielle, and I'm guessing I won't be able to separate Sayen from her, which is a shame because with her enhancements, she's very useful."

"But that means only you, Carl, and Ozment will be there. That isn't enough. You need me."

The kid was right. Though she hated the thought of taking someone so young into such a dangerous situation, they would need everyone they could get. And Makey seemed to have learned his lesson since Antarctica. She didn't think he would disobey another order so lightly again.

"Well..." she said, and Makey's expression brightened. "We'll see." His expression fell. "How about I give you some training, and if you do well enough, you can come."

"That sounds great," he exclaimed. "Can we start right now?"

"Not yet," Jas replied. "We'll wait until the sun swings round into the yard. It'll make the laser beams less easy to see from a distance. You showed you were a good shot when you and Carl saved my life on Dawn, but some target practice never hurts. For now, go to your room and do the exercises I showed you to build up your core strength. I'll call you when it's time."

Makey didn't need telling twice. He was gone in a moment. Carl caught the door as it swung to behind the kid and closed it. He took Makey's place next to Jas and spread his arms along the back of the seat. Neither said anything, but the silence between them felt comfortable.

After a little while, Carl said, "I was talking to Ozment about his farm."

"Oh yeah?"

"Yeah. Sounds like a great place. They grow all kinds of crops down there. Keep goats and pigs too. Got a good set up."

Carl seemed to be leading up to something, and Jas wondered what it was. Was he planning on going there when this business with the Shadows was over?

"Seems like a nice guy," Carl went on.

He was on edge about something. Jas could tell from the way his accent had gotten stronger. She liked the sound of his Australian drawl. It gave her a warm feeling.

"Ozment?" she said. "I was suspicious of him at first, but I think you're right. He's okay."

"I suppose you and he get along pretty well. With him being another Martian, I mean."

They had both been looking out into the view from the back yard, which was of a derelict building site that had been abandoned, leaving only the foundation. At Carl's sentence, however, Jas turned to look at him. He continued to gaze steadily out and wouldn't meet her eyes.

"Oh Carl, don't be an idiot."

He finally looked at her. "What do you mean?"

"I like Ozment, but not like that." She sighed. "The last time I got close to someone, I ended up bashing in his Shadow's head with a rock. Even if I did want something more with Ozment—which I don't—this isn't the right time. A lot of people are going to lose the ones they love before this is all over. It doesn't make a lot of sense to open ourselves up to more hurt."

"Yeah, I suppose you're right."

Jas returned her gaze to the distance, and another silence fell. The sun's beams crept slowly into the yard, lighting up the weeds and the insects that flew and danced among them. After a little while, Jas leaned her head against Carl's shoulder, and he wrapped his arm around her. They stayed in that position, neither saying a word, until Makey burst out of the house, asking breathlessly if it was time for target practice yet.

12

———

The next day, as Jas was teaching Makey some hand-to-hand fighting techniques, murmuring voices came from Erielle's room, growing louder. Soon, shouting could be heard. Erielle was arguing with her doctor friend.

"For krat's sake, see sense, woman," shouted the man. "You were always stubborn, but this is ridiculous."

Erielle retorted, "Just forget it, okay? You'd never understand."

"And what's *that* supposed to mean?"

"I said, forget it."

"Forget it? After I've brought you back from the brink of death? After I've ventured into this gangland for you? Do you know the cabs won't even come down this street? They stop at the end, and I have to walk the rest of the way, risking life and limb at the hands of your underworld thugs."

"Hey," exclaimed Erielle, "don't talk about my friends that way."

"Did your friends save your life? Are your friends

offering to operate on you and give you back the ability to walk? When I heard you were in trouble, I hadn't seen you for twenty years. I didn't know if you were alive or dead. But I came. I came because I was told you needed me. But apparently not. Apparently, I'm not one of your *friends*. That's it, Erielle. It's over. I suggest you forget my number, because the next time I receive an anonymous call, I won't be answering it."

Loud footsteps rang from the hallway, and the house resounded as the front door was slammed shut.

Makey was lying on the floor, where Jas had thrown him. He raised himself up on his elbows. "I don't think he'll be back."

"No, I don't think so either," Jas agreed. "But Erielle sounds a lot better. I'll go in to see her later. Come on, get up. Now, you work the same move on me."

Makey stood and waited for Jas to run at him. When she did, he grappled her and hooked his foot behind her ankle. She landed on her back. "Well done," she told him from the floor. "That should work on someone taller than you who has some momentum going. You can use that to unbalance them and—"

Sayen flung open the door and marched in. She threw herself into a chair and crossed her arms. "Oh, sorry," she said when she noticed Jas and Makey. "You carry on. I just had to get away from Erielle. She's driving me insane. I've tried everything I can think of to get her to change her mind, but she's adamant. She'd rather spend the rest of her life scooting around on a board with wheels than get her legs fixed. Can you believe it?"

"I don't understand it either," Jas said, "but if she doesn't want the surgery, what can you do?"

"But you should see her legs. They're healing up all right, but they look awful. There's hardly any tissue left where the laser hit her. It isn't only a matter of her never walking again. If she doesn't have treatment, she's going to be in pain for the rest of her life. She doesn't say anything, but she's in constant, severe pain all the time already. You can see it on her face. I think she hardly sleeps at night because of it. Ozment's been doping her up with kratom, but I don't think it's enough. Who would choose to live like that?"

"Most of the Dawntowners would," said Makey. "The older ones, anyway. The first generation colonists, they were almost all like that. I never really understood it either, but Erielle's way of thinking isn't that unusual to me."

Sayen shook her head sadly. "I just don't get it."

"Me either," Jas said. "But don't forget she grew up in a different time from us. That seems to have something to do with it. Today's generation of underworlders don't seem to hold the same strong opinions about global control through technology. They seem to be mostly naturals who can't get jobs, or addicts. I think the old Green Earthers developed their ideas when the world was changing rapidly, and people had to decide whether or not to continue with technological development. People like Erielle only see the bad that technology brought with it."

Sayen sighed. "She's told me what happened that opened her eyes to the things she hates about the world today, and it was terrible. But I still don't understand. If she allows her friend to operate, it doesn't make her a participant in the way our society's run. It doesn't mean she's doing those things herself."

"For some people," Makey said, "it's the same thing. My da thinks he's tainted if he touches anything 'unnatural' as he puts it. He has to go and wash himself afterward. It's strange, but it's the way he thinks."

Ozment came into the room. "Erielle's asking for you, Sayen."

She got up to leave.

"Wait a minute," Jas said. "We're setting off tomorrow. Are you coming, or do you want to stay here? We can't take the minister with us. We need someone to guard her for another few days. And Erielle..."

Her expression sad, Sayen said, "I can't leave her. Not yet." She went out.

"We need to talk," Jas said to Ozment. "Are you still on board with helping us steal a Shadow scanner?"

"Yes, I am." He rubbed his hands together. "It's been a while since I did anything downright criminal."

"You don't count growing kratom as criminal?" Jas asked, her eyebrows raised.

"I'm nothing but a simple farmer," Ozment replied. "I can't help it if my crops have special properties." He winked at Makey.

"Hey, no corrupting the kid."

"Wouldn't dream of it."

Jas narrowed her eyes at him. "So, let's figure out our route, and what we need to take."

"I've got the route figured out already. We can stop overnight at a national park. I can park the truck behind some RVs where it won't attract too much attention. We'll blend in with the tourists. It's busy there this time of year."

"Sounds good. We'll have to leave some weapons here for Sayen. She'll be by herself with an invalid and a hostage to protect. I wouldn't put it past Durfy and his clan to figure out where we are. I don't like leaving her."

"We can give her plenty of guns," said Ozment. "Once

we're inside the cargo warehouse, there shouldn't be much need for fighting. The guards will be on the perimeter. My truck will get us through that. Smash, grab, and run." He grinned. "Like the old days."

13

They came from across the abandoned building site in the early hours of the morning. Jas was asleep. She'd tied Bathsheba to the other bed in the room. She hadn't liked doing it. Over the days that the minister had been living with them, Jas had grown accustomed to her. She didn't think she was a bad person, just misguided and out of touch, and perhaps too sure of herself. Jas believed she genuinely hadn't known that the Shadows had infiltrated Earth to the extent they had. As she fell asleep, Jas had been looking forward to the day they could let the older woman go.

The first Jas heard of the underworlders' attack was the tinkle of glass breaking. As her eyes flicked open, she reached for the blaster next to her bed. Her waking brain tried to compute where the sound had come from. It seemed to have been from the kitchen, which was below Jas's room. Carl and Makey shared the bedroom next door, Ozment had his own room at the front of the house, and Sayen and Erielle were in the living room.

Jas was already up and moving toward the door. The

sound of someone breaking a window hadn't woken the minister. She lay on her back on top of her covers, wearing the same kaftan she'd worn when she'd been kidnapped. Jas contemplated untying her for her own safety, but decided against it. She was safer exactly as she was. If she ran off into the underworld territory at that hour of the night, she wouldn't last five minutes.

It had to be Durfy's gang. But were they there for Bathsheba, or had someone discovered that Erielle was there? Had Durfy come to assassinate the underworld leader so that he could take her place? Jas's stomach tightened. Erielle was entirely unable to defend herself, and Sayen was unarmed.

As she left the room, the door on her right opened. Carl emerged. Makey followed. They'd been woken by the noise too.

"Wake Ozment," Jas told Makey in an undertone. On bare feet, she went downstairs, her gun at the ready, Carl behind her.

All was dark. No streetlights were working, and the night was cloudy. Jas paused at the bottom stair, peering into the velvet blackness. She held her breath. Was someone in the hallway already? Watching her?

A slow creak came from the kitchen door. Jas was thankful for the rusty hinges. She lifted her weapon to fire, but she hesitated. What if it wasn't an underworlder, but Sayen, who had gone into the kitchen for a drink of water in the night? What if the sound she'd heard had been Sayen dropping a glass?

But the door to the living room began to open, and Jas knew where Sayen was. She fired at the dark figure emerging from the kitchen. There was a scream followed by shouting. The form that Jas had shot thumped to the floor.

Scuffling and the sound of furniture being overturned was loud in the house.

The living room door had closed at the first shot. Jas kept her gun trained on the kitchen, but no one else emerged. She glanced up at Carl, who was on the steps above her, also waiting for the next move from the underworlders.

Jas was blinded by something on her left. A laser beam had shot right through the front door, narrowly missing her head. Her retinas burned, and she could see nothing but a red glow. "I'm blinded," she gasped to Carl. The hiss of his weapon told her he'd fired back through the door. He pushed her to one side.

"Get upstairs," he said. "Check on the minister. Ozment's here."

Groping on her hands and knees, Jas climbed the steps and felt her way along the hallway, trying to blink away the scarlet glare. Finding the doorknob by touch, she went into her bedroom. The minister was awake and asking her what was happening.

"The underworlders have found us," Jas replied. She searched for the bonds that tied the woman to the bed and began to untie the knots.

"They've come for me again?" Bathsheba asked nervously. "What if I tell them what they want to know? They'd let me go then, wouldn't they?"

"No, I don't think so," Jas said. She'd noticed the deep hatred the underworlders bore toward the woman, even if the minister hadn't. It wasn't only their hope that she could lead them to hard drugs that drove their desire to capture her. She didn't want to frighten her, but she didn't imagine Bathsheba would last long in Durfy's hands.

No more sounds of fighting were coming from downstairs. It looked like the underworlders had given up their attack for the moment. Jas's sight was also returning. Dark gray shapes were appearing from the fading red. Bathsheba's anxious face shone palely in the scant light. Jas was wondering what to do next—should they go on the offensive and drive the underworlders away, or should they wait until dawn—when someone ran up the stairs and along the hallway. Carl burst into the room.

"The kitchen's on fire," he exclaimed. "It's out of control. We've gotta get out."

"Krat. They're forcing us to leave. They're going to pick us off one by one the minute we go outside." Jas was untying the final knot at the minister's wrist.

The woman ripped her hand free and clutched at Jas. "Help me. I don't want to die."

"Then do as I say," Jas replied. "Is Ozment helping Erielle?" she asked Carl.

"Yes."

"Stick with Makey, then, Carl. Don't let him out of your sight. Tell everyone to wait in the hallway. We're coming. "

"Stay safe, Jas," Carl said, and he was gone.

She grabbed the bag of weapons. Everything else, she left. "Put on your shoes," she told Bathsheba. "Come with me and don't leave my side, no matter what happens."

The woman took Jas's last instruction literally. She clutched her arm in an almost painful grip. Jas swung the bag of weapons over her shoulder with her other hand and together they left the bedroom. Smoke from the kitchen made the dark house utterly impenetrable to sight. Jas reached for the banister rail. From below came the sound of coughing. They had only seconds to get out before smoke inhalation rendered everyone unconscious.

Bathsheba was gibbering frightened nonsense at her

side as they felt their way quickly downstairs. "Calm down," Jas hissed. She was worried the woman would do something stupid in her terror and get them all killed.

"Ozment," she said into the choking smoke. "You've got to get your truck open. You'll have to go first. I'll cover you."

"I have to carry Erielle," he replied.

"No," came Sayen's voice, "I can do it. I can. Trust me."

"Okay," Ozment said.

Jas was at the front door. She slid her hand across it, found the handle and turned it. As she raised her weapon to fire through the gap, she was thrown roughly aside. It was Bathsheba. She ran out, shouting, "Don't shoot. Don't shoot. I'll—"

The buzz of laser fire was followed by a terrible shriek. The minister collapsed. Jas gasped, but she'd seen from where the underworlders were firing. She returned fire, shouting at Ozment, "Go. Now."

The large man sped over the short distance to his truck and was inside in a heartbeat. The laser proof steel shields rose up and slid into place around the cab. "Sayen, Erielle," shouted Jas, firing again into the darkness.

Sayen ran low across the front yard, carrying the crippled woman over her shoulder in a fireman's lift.

"Carl, fire at that alleyway. I'll take this side. Let's go."

Jas, Makey, and Carl raced to Ozment's truck. On the way, Jas glimpsed Bathsheba. She was on her back, her stomach and chest open, burned, and bleeding, her eyes flickering closed. Then the image was gone. Arms were pulling Jas into Ozment's cab. The engine was already running. The door was slammed shut, and they were driving into the night.

14

———

Carl leaned an arm on the open window of the truck and watched the countryside speed past. Though the cab was large, it wasn't meant to hold six people, and he was hot, cramped, and uncomfortable. Erielle was lying in the narrow space at the back, but everyone else was crammed across the long bucket seat at the front. It didn't help that the air-conditioning seemed to have given out under the strain of trying to cool six bodies. Only the breeze pouring in the window gave some relief.

"How long now?" Carl asked Ozment and immediately regretted it. He sounded like a whiny kid. The fact was, as well as the confined conditions bothering him, he hated it when someone else was driving.

"Couple more hours," came the reply.

Carl couldn't wait to arrive at the national park that was to be their halfway stop on the way to the spaceport. He was sure the others felt the same. The general mood was very low. Jas was deeply cut up about the death of the minister, Carl could tell. He didn't think she should blame herself so much. If the woman hadn't been trying to brush the problem of the Shadows under the carpet, she and a lot more people would still be alive.

Sayen had a line between her eyes that never seemed to go away. She was worrying about Erielle, no doubt. The underworlder wasn't really well enough to be moved. Ozment was concentrating on the road. Makey was the only one who seemed relatively cheerful.

They'd been driving through flat farmland for hours, but the mountains that had been far distant were drawing close, and the fields had given way to sparse woods. The air outside grew cooler as dusk drew on, and they drove into the shadow of the trees. Slowly, the road began to slope upward.

"Can we stop for some water?" Sayen asked Ozment.

"Sure. There's a camping store along here somewhere, if I remember right. We can have a rest stop and stock up. We'll need sleeping bags. Gets cold up in the mountains at night."

"We can't pay for anything," said Jas. "Erielle's crew stole our credchips, but we couldn't use them anyway. The Shadows know that we know about them. They're looking for us."

"Don't worry. I'll pay. You can pay me back with labor on my farm." He turned and winked to show that he was joking, but his words caused an ache of homesickness in Carl. He would have given a lot to be back on his parents' farm, dusting crops with Flux beside him in the cockpit. He hoped the little fella was doing okay in his absence. He wished he could call him.

"What do you grow, apart from kratom, I mean?" Jas asked Ozment.

"Bananas, avocado, watermelon, guava, eggplants,

mangoes, papayas, oranges, peaches, peanuts, sweetcorn, tomatoes, squash, beans, passionfruit, lychees, lettuce—"

"Whoa, you grow a lot of stuff."

"Yeah, I don't only deal in narcotics, you know. I run a mean sideline in fruit and vegetables too."

His joke broke the tension somewhat, and the cooler temperatures and prospect of an imminent escape from the close confines of the truck's cab also sparked a shift in mood.

"Do you drive this route when you go to the city?" Jas asked.

"No. It's pretty, but the freeway is faster. I've been here for a break a few times, though. The road's wide enough for the truck."

"Is it busy this time of year?"

"It didn't use to be, but lately it's become popular with alien tourists. It's within a few hours of the spaceport, and they can spend a day or so here in a typical Earth landscape before heading off on a tour of the major sites."

Makey sat up. "Aliens? I've only ever seen the haidiren. What are they like?"

"You see all kinds of weird and wonderful creatures up there. Should be interesting for you."

Ozment's comment also piqued Carl's interest. Though he'd visited more planets than he could easily count, shuttle pilots on prospecting missions were generally required to remain with their spacecraft in case of an emergency evacuation. And his parents' farm was far from the tourist areas where visiting aliens were commonly seen.

"Won't we stand out?" asked Jas. "We hardly look like tourists. The last thing we want to do is attract attention."

"Maybe a little," Ozment replied. "But I don't see how that can be helped. We'd stick out more at a regular truck stop, that's for sure. There aren't many truckers who try to squeeze six people, including an invalid, into their cabs. Besides, the only authorities up there are the rangers. They see all kinds of folks and don't pay them any mind as long as they follow the rules. We should be okay."

Carl settled back in his seat and let the refreshing air from the window cool the sweat on his neck and chest. In another few minutes a single story cabin appeared on the side of the road. The camping store had parking space for RVs around the back. Carl, Jas, and Ozment went into the store while Sayen and Makey stretched their legs.

A warm, musty, pleasant scent of wood greeted them inside the camping store. It was filled floor to ceiling with equipment for basic through luxury camping. A red-cheeked young woman sat behind the counter watching an interface on the wall. Jas and Ozment went to look at the sleeping bags, and Carl went over to see the screen, which was showing the latest vidnews. He'd been attracted by a flash of a building that looked familiar. As he watched, he found his suspicion was correct. The screen displayed an aerial view of the Global Government Security Head-quarters.

"Can I help you, sir?" asked the woman as she noticed Carl standing there.

"No, thanks. I'm waiting for my friends."

An image of Bathsheba Dubois appeared, looking very different from when Carl had last seen her. She was in a Government meeting with other ministers, looking commanding and dignified. He remembered her fury at being kidnapped, and her descent into terror of Durfy's crew.

Another image appeared. It was an older man with white hair and a beard, closely clipped. He was well-dressed in a tailored navy suit. The unseen anchor announced that since her disappearance, the security minister's secretary had been representing her at meetings, but as the police were no further with their investigation to find the missing official, a stand-in would be chosen as a temporary replacement.

The older man fitted the description of the Shadow Bernie that Sayen given them. So a Shadow had been taking part in Government meetings. Carl wondered if whoever was in line to be Bathsheba's replacement was also a Shadow. They had to contact the Transgalactic Council urgently before the aliens got any further in their takeover of Earth.

"Isn't it terrible?" the assistant asked Carl. "That poor woman. I wonder what they did to her? I guess there's no hope she's still alive after all this time."

"What did who do to her?"

"Didn't you hear? It's been all over the news."

"No, I've, er, been out in the woods for a couple of weeks."

"The police suspect she was kidnapped by that old Green Earthers cult that was supposed to have died out decades ago. It was before my time, but I heard they were pretty crazy. They say the cult's been revived, and they've turned to terrorism to try to get their way."

"Green Earthers, huh? They were a little before my time too. Did they publish their demands?"

"Not that I've heard, but the authorities seem pretty sure it was them."

Ozment and Jas appeared, their arms full of sleeping bags, bottles of water, and packets of snack food. After Ozment paid, they left.

"You've got a credchip embedded then?" Jas asked him as they went back to the truck.

"The farm's legit," he said, "even if not everything we grow on it is. There's only so much you can trade vegetables for."

"Traitor," said Jas with a wry smile.

15

S ayen fixed two sleeping bags together and slept next to Erielle that night to share her body warmth with the injured woman. She couldn't stop worrying about her. Though her old doctor friend had saved her life, she was still far from better and not in any fit state to be traveling for hours in a truck.

Erielle never mentioned it, but the underworlder was clearly in a lot of pain. Ozment had supplied her with kratom pellets that kept her in a sedated haze most of the time, but she was often pale and sweaty before it was safe for her to take another dose. Erielle had feeling in her legs but it was impossible for her to move them. When they were accidentally moved or even touched by others, she would cry out. Apart from requests for water and help with other basic needs, she said very little. Sayen wondered how long it would be before they could go somewhere safe, where Erielle could rest and get better.

She tried to make herself comfortable on the floor at the back of the truck, where she and the others had lain down after pulling into the campsite after dark. Ozment had left the truck door ajar to let in a little air. After hours of agitated fidgeting, Erielle was finally breathing in the slow, steady manner that indicated she was asleep. Sayen needed some exercise, however, before sleep would come to her.

After unfastening the sleeping bag as quietly as she could, she got up and padded across to the door, where she slipped on her shoes. She dropped onto the asphalt of the car park and headed for a trail that led up into the trees. It was a clear night, and the moon's beams and starlight made it easy to see without the help of her night vision.

Sayen hiked up the sloping trail for a kilometer or so, enjoying the freedom and the short respite from the harrowing events of the previous few days. Now that she had the leisure to go over everything in her mind, she could hardly believe all that had happened since she'd been captured by the Shadows at her workplace. It had been only a couple of weeks since she'd left home by heli.

Thinking of her home made her wonder what was happening to her parents. Carl and Jas had said they were afraid to leave their estate. She hoped they were safe from the Shadows there. They had to be worrying about her, too. A sudden realization made her gasp. When Erielle had destroyed her tracker, the signal from it must have disappeared. Did her parents think she was dead?

Her eyes filled with tears. She'd never wanted to upset them or make them worry about her. She wished there was a way she could get a message to them to let them know she was okay, but she couldn't think of a method that wouldn't put either her or them in danger.

Sayen was so preoccupied with her thoughts, she didn't notice the aliens approaching her on the trail ahead until they were almost on top of her. They seemed to suddenly loom up out of nowhere. More than two meters tall and wide, four insectoid aliens bore down on her, black silhouettes against the starry night sky.

She gave a small scream, and the aliens stopped, seeming to only just notice her.

"I do apologize," one of them said. "We did not detect your scent among the many strange and wonderful odors of this environment." As it spoke, a second set of sharp mandibles protruded from the outer pair and dripped with mucus.

"Oh my word," gasped Sayen, stumbling backward.

"Please do not be alarmed. We are entirely harmless. Our species is noted for its natural pacifism, in fact. But we understand that our appearance is alarming to humans. That is why we are exploring this landscape at night, while most humans are sleeping. Please forgive us for frightening you."

Sayen swallowed and took a deep breath. Her heart was racing. "It's okay. You didn't scare me a lot." She was lying, but the creature seemed genuinely mortified that they had given her a shock. "Do...do you like it here? Have you been on Earth long?"

"From what we've seen of it so far," said the alien, "we like it very much. This area is particularly attractive. You must be very proud of your planet."

"Thanks. You're very kind," Sayen replied, slipping into the formal small talk she'd learned to use when speaking to important friends and associates of her parents. The whole situation felt slightly bizarre. "I, er, I hope you enjoy the rest of your vacation."

"Thank you. I am sure we will. It has been very pleasant to make your acquaintance."

"Likewise," Sayen said. "Well, I guess I'll be going."

"We hope you enjoy your walk," said the alien.

"Thank you. I'm sure I shall." She stepped to one side and suppressed a shudder as the aliens passed by, the claws on the ends of their ten pairs of legs faintly scratching against the wood chip path. She remained where she was until the creatures disappeared around a bend in the trail. Exhaling deeply, she went on.

At a high point on the track, the trees thinned out enough to allow a view of the surrounding countryside. Clusters of tiny artificial lights marked the nearby towns on the plain below, and the roads that joined them were traced with the minuscule moving headlights of cars and trucks. Sayen squatted down for a while, her arms wrapped around her knees, as she wondered which of the houses and vehicles contained not humans, but Shadow clones.

After a while, it occurred to her that Erielle might have woken and be in need of another dose of kratom. She returned down the trail to the car park and crept into the truck. The underworlder was sleeping as soundly as she'd been when Sayen left her. She climbed inside the warm sleeping bag and settled down, finally able to drift off to sleep.

She was woken the following day by the sounds of movement and quiet voices. Erielle was already awake. She'd managed to sit up and pull herself backward on her arms so that she could lean against the truck wall. She gave a wan half-smile as she looked into Sayen's sleep-filled eyes.

Sayen yawned. "How are you feeling?"

"A little better. You should get up soon if you want to get some breakfast."

Sayen pushed back the sleeping bag and sat up. Jas,

Ozment, and Carl were sitting cross-legged next to the truck door, which was wide open. Brilliant sunlight streamed in, and the sound of birdsong was loud.

"Where's Makey?" she asked Erielle. "Has he gone to take a shower?" She hoped there were showers at this place.

"No, I sent him on an errand."

"What kind of errand?"

"You'll see."

"Time to get up," Ozment said as he noticed she was awake. "We're leaving soon. We've got to get to the spaceport while it's still daylight so that we can get a good look at the place."

"Okay, okay," Sayen replied. "Have you eaten?" she asked Erielle.

"Yes. There's some left, but like Ozment said, be quick."

"I'll take you to the bathroom first."

"I don't think there'll be any need for that."

Makey climbed inside, carrying two long, straight branches. "This wood's great," he said. "I heard about trees, but I never imagined how useful they could be. Life on Dawn would have been so much easier if trees had grown there." He handed a knife to Ozment, who slipped it into a sheath at his side.

"Will these do, do you think?" he asked Erielle, holding up the branches for her inspection. He'd cut them to the same length, which was somewhat longer than a meter. At the top of each the branch split into a fork.

"Oh, you got him to make you crutches," Sayen exclaimed. "Wait, let me find something we can wrap around the ends for padding."

When she'd made the crutches as comfortable as she could, she carried Erielle to the door, where Makey held them upright for her. Slowly, she lowered the woman until her armpits rested on the branch forks. Her right leg was less damaged than her left, and Erielle gingerly put her weight on it while trying to take most of the strain on her arms.

She let out a gasp of pain and fell forward. Makey caught her and held onto her while she tried again. Once more, she couldn't take the pain, and she collapsed.

"That's enough for now," Sayen said. "Have a rest, and we can try again later."

"No, I want to do this."

Unable to hold it back, Erielle cried out as she hopped forward one step. She fell down. Neither Sayen nor Makey were quick enough to catch her.

"Erielle, this is stupid," Sayen said. "There's no need for this. Let me carry you."

Erielle glared at her from the ground. "Makey, help me up, please." She slipped the crutches under her arms, and the young man pulled her to her feet.

The next time she tried to walk, she managed two steps before crashing to the ground again.

"Erielle—" A hand gripped Sayen's shoulder. She turned to see Jas.

"She's doing pretty well, don't you think?" Jas asked.

"No, she's going to hurt herself. We can get her some proper crutches or a wheelchair. And it's much too soon—"

"Sayen, why not let her do it her way? I thought you hated your parents being overprotective of you."

"This is different. My parents are totally over the top. I just don't want her to hurt herself. I care about her."

"I know. Look, it's nearly time to go. Eat something and get ready. We've got five or six hours' driving ahead of us."

16

A heat shimmer hung over the spaceport landing pad. Jas squinted in the glaring sunlight at the cargo bay. They'd parked the truck a little way down the road.

Jas wished she had some binoculars to see more detail. Then she remembered the weapons they'd brought from Erielle's place. She dug into the bag and pulled out an old-fashioned rifle with a sight. Peering through the crosshairs, she could see close up the perimeter fence around the spaceport, the massive shuttle hangars, the passenger buildings, and the warehouse that stored the cargo waiting to be loaded onto flights or ready for pickup.

If Bathsheba Dubois had been telling the truth, the shuttle flight carrying the Shadow scanners would be arriving at 7 pm. At 8:15—to allow time for offloading and transfer to the storage area—anonymous governmental trucks would pick up the scanners for distribution to the various spaceports around the world that handled deep space arrivals. They would have a window of about half an hour to break in and steal a scanner.

"What can you see?" asked Makey, who was crouched beside her on the rise that overlooked the spaceport.

"I can't see guards anywhere, for one thing," she replied. Turning to Carl, she asked, "You've spent a lot of time hanging around restricted areas in spaceports. Is it normal to have no guards?"

"It's not a military installation. They aren't expecting to be attacked. There are probably a few guards on site, but not many, and they wouldn't spend all day patrolling."

"That's good for us," Jas said, "but what about protection from theft? There have to be some valuable shipments that pass through."

Carl nodded. "The storage areas are sealed up pretty tight. Only cleared personnel can get access after retinal and voice checks. What we have to worry about are motion sensors. While the spaceport's in operation, they're turned off because the workers are constantly moving cargo in and out of storage. But overnight, the motion sensors are activated. They're trigger alarms, and they shoot whatever moving object they detect."

"Krat," Jas said.

"But if we break in while the place is open, these sensors won't be activated, will they?" Makey asked.

"Not right away," said Carl, "but the minute they realize what's happening, you can be sure as hell that system will be the first thing they reach for. Which means we've got to be fast. As soon as we're sure the scanners are inside the warehouse, we should break in, take one, and get out of there."

"Do we know where in the warehouse they'll put the scanners?" Makey asked.

Jas gazed through the crosshairs again at the huge spaceport. "Nope."

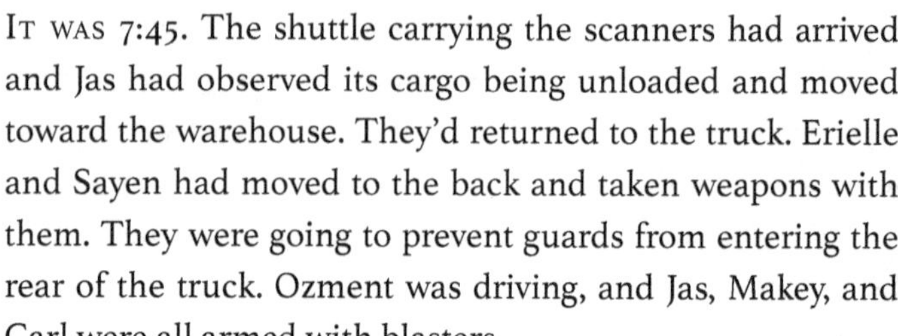

IT WAS 7:45. The shuttle carrying the scanners had arrived and Jas had observed its cargo being unloaded and moved toward the warehouse. They'd returned to the truck. Erielle and Sayen had moved to the back and taken weapons with them. They were going to prevent guards from entering the rear of the truck. Ozment was driving, and Jas, Makey, and Carl were all armed with blasters.

Jas's greatest fear was that they wouldn't be able to find the scanners before the motion sensors were turned on, or that the sensors would automatically activate the minute they broke into the warehouse. If that happened, they wouldn't stand a chance. They would be trapped inside the truck, unless...

"Are you sure this is tough enough to break through the warehouse wall?" Carl asked Ozment.

"Should be," he replied. "But I can't say as I've ever tried. Buckle up, everyone." He was driving at the speed of the traffic on the approach to the spaceport, but soon he would have to veer off the road and across the open land surrounding it.

"Hey, listen up, take one of these," Jas said, pulling more guns from her cache and handing them to Carl, Makey, and Ozment.

"Aren't these a little outdated?" Ozment asked as he took a weapon from her.

She'd given them each a pistol that fired rounds and not the laser beams of modern weapons. "Yes, they're old, but they might be just what we need. The motion sensors are probably laser-proofed, but they might not be bulletproof. Here." She gave them each a magazine of bullets. "There aren't many. They probably don't even make these anymore. So every shot is going to count."

They were nearly at the spaceport. "Okay, this is it," Jas said. "Remember, we find a scanner, get it in the back of the truck, then get the hell out of there."

The truck swerved and began to judder as Ozment left the road, went down a bank, and across rough dirt and rocks. They were about a minute from the spaceport. Jas wondered if anyone had noticed them yet. They were thirty seconds away. The perimeter fence and the corrugated metal wall of the warehouse were rushing up toward them.

Ozment pressed a switch, and steel walls flew up around the cab and slotted into place, leaving only a narrow slit in front of the driver. The juddering was violent as Ozment increased speed. "Get ready," he shouted.

As they struck the fence and then the warehouse, Jas was thrown forward. A great rending and tearing of metal could be heard all around. When it stopped, she opened her eyes. "Are we in?"

Ozment peered through the slit. "We're in. Go."

Jas threw her door open and leapt out. She landed awkwardly on broken boxes of goods strewn around the cab. "Be careful," she called to the others. At the far end of the warehouse, workers were running away. Automated forklift trucks in the warehouse aisles continued to operate, lifting and carrying stored items.

Only the cab of the truck had made it through the wall. If they were going to load up a scanner, they needed access to the rear doors. "Ozment," Jas called. "You've got to pull the whole truck in."

Carl and Makey were setting off on the search for the scanner. As Jas joined them, the truck engine revved, and the warehouse was filled with deafening noise as Ozment destroyed more of its wall and knocked down a massive shelf of goods to bring the rear of the truck inside.

Where were the scanners? They probably had only seconds before someone thought to activate the motion sensors. "Let's check up near the entrance," Jas said. "The scanners were only supposed to be here a little while before they were picked up."

They moved down an aisle. In front of them was a forklift, trundling in their direction, a pallet of boxes balanced on its forks. Suddenly, a laser beam flashed out, and the truck burst apart. The boxes fell and smashed, spilling their contents.

"Krat," Jas said. She froze. Makey and Carl also stopped.

"What do we do now?" Makey asked.

"Wait."

Jas's eyes were on the forklifts in their aisle. Another beam flashed out and hit a moving truck, and this time she saw the motion sensor that was responsible. It was on the ceiling, moving to fire again as it detected the final surviving forklift in their aisle. As the third beam shone, Jas lifted her weapon, aimed, and shot. A massive bang echoed around the warehouse, and the sensor exploded. Plastic and metal debris rained down. "Makey, you spot and take out the motion sensors. We don't have long before they run out of targets except for us. Carl, let's find this kratting scanner."

They set off. Shots rang out as the kid traced the beams flashing from the ceiling. Jas and Carl ran low and kept to the sides of the aisles. Jas hoped that the forklifts would attract more attention than them from the motion sensors.

At the end of the warehouse, near the open doors, a couple dozen boxes shaped like large coffins were stacked.

"You reckon that's them?" asked Carl, who had spotted the boxes too.

"Got to be, don't you think? We'll just have to take a chance. It isn't like they would have labeled them."

Another laser beam flashed out, this time low down from the warehouse entrance. Guards had arrived and spotted them.

"Krat," Jas said. "I hate to do this, but..." She pulled a grenade from her jacket pocket, set it and tossed it through the doors. As it exploded, she and Carl ran toward the boxes. She grabbed the end of one, and Carl grabbed the other end. They slid it off the pile, but it was so heavy, they couldn't hold onto it. The box fell to the floor. "We'll have to push it," Jas said. "Quick."

They both pushed and dragged the box back toward the aisle. Right next to Jas's hand, a laser beam burnt the container. She spun around to see a guard ducking back behind the door. She fired her old-fashioned propulsion weapon. The round pierced the laser-proofed door, and a cry sounded.

They reached the relative safety of the aisle, but the box was so heavy, they were only inching it along. Makey fired. The guards had entered the warehouse. If they didn't find a faster way of getting the box to the truck, the place would be swarming with them. As Jas grunted and strained, she glanced up and caught sight of a figure that gave her hope. Sayen was racing toward them. She'd left the truck and come to help.

But a motion sensor detected her. Its beam caught her side, and she staggered and fell. Jas shot the sensor. Sayen got up and continued toward them more slowly. When she reached them, Jas saw her left arm and back had been burned. Her face was twisted in pain.

"Let's move this thing," she gasped, and she placed her right hand next to Jas's. With her help, the box slid easily along. As they made their way back to the truck, Makey fired at the guards that were trying to pursue them.

Ozment also approached to lend a hand. "The truck's rear doors are open. We've just gotta get this inside."

They were nearly there. Behind the truck was a gaping hole where Ozment had driven the truck through the wall. Jas saw movement. "Krat. The guards have come around this side." A beam flashed from inside the truck, and a guard fell. Erielle was firing at them. Another guard appeared and was caught on the shoulder by a beam from Erielle's gun.

"Makey, cover us," Jas ordered.

He fired shot after shot through the hole while the other four hoisted the box into the truck. In another moment, the doors were closed and they were back in the cab. Ozment reversed the truck out of the warehouse, buckling and breaking more of the wall. The guards outside fired, but their laser beams sizzled uselessly.

They rocked and swayed as Ozment forced the truck around in a tight curve to get back to the road. Then they were out in the traffic, heading away from the spaceport.

17

———

Whoops and hollers filled the cab as they sped from the spaceport. As soon as they were a safe distance away, they stopped the truck and opened the box. Inside they found exactly what they'd hoped for. They'd done it. They'd stolen a scanner. Sayen and Ozment helped Erielle into the cab and they set off once more. Jas leaned back in her seat, and for the first time in days, she relaxed.

They still had to capture a Shadow, and that wouldn't be easy, but they were much further along with their plan than they had been only a day previously.

Ozment was driving with a huge grin on his face.

"You seem pretty pleased with yourself," she said to him.

"It always feels good when you stick it to the man," he replied.

"Where are we going now?" Makey asked.

Jas realized that they hadn't even considered their next step. There could be no going back to Erielle's safe house, even if anything remained of it after the fire. Durfy and his associates wouldn't be pleased by their return.

"You're coming with me to my farm," said Ozment. "I thought that was obvious."

"Great," said Makey.

"Yeah, thanks, mate," Carl said. "Great idea. We can rest up for a while, and Erielle can get better."

Sayen nodded in satisfaction.

A shadow flickered over the cab, as if something had passed by overhead. Over the sound of the truck's engine, Jas thought she heard a high-pitched whine.

"What was that?" Makey asked.

"Sounded like a heli," Sayen said.

The truck shuddered as something hit its roof.

"Krat. We're being fired at," exclaimed Ozment. On the dashboard, in the screens showing the rear- and side-views, the dark shapes of two helis could be seen, hovering over the truck like mosquitoes in search of blood.

"Carl, take over," Ozment said. "I'll deal with them."

Jas remembered the false roof of the truck that Ozment had told her about, and the 'toy' he had up there.

Ozment and Carl awkwardly swapped seats, and Ozment crawled into the back of the cab and opened the hatch. He disappeared up the dark tunnel leading to the roof. The truck shuddered again, and Carl fought to keep it on the road.

The dark countryside was speeding past. Jas gripped a handle over the window to keep her balance. She pressed a button, and the plexiglass retracted into its slot. Leaning out, she saw the two helis overhead. They were flying erratically, as if the pilots were unused to the controls. *As if they were being flown by newly formed Shadows.*

An arc of fire spat from the truck roof, and the rotor blade of one of the helis flew off, spinning crazily down before it hit the road. Sparks erupted from it as it skittered along, and cars swerved to avoid it. A dull rumble and flash of flame signaled the damaged heli crashing into a field at their rear.

"He got one," Jas exclaimed. She was aiming at the remaining heli, but its haphazard movement made it difficult to follow. The shot she fired went wide. Something erupted from the heli's base, and a third shudder ran through the truck, followed by a loud bang. The heli had scored a direct hit, but it was firing at the largest target—the truck's roof, probably aiming for the weapon Ozment was firing. *Better that than the wheels*, Jas thought. If the Shadows took them out, it would be game over, but her stomach clenched at the thought of the man in the false roof.

Another line of fire flew up from the truck. A hole appeared in the center of the second heli a moment before it was consumed in a ball of flames. The fiery ball hit the road behind them and rolled away, leaving a trail of burning debris.

"Second heli down," exclaimed Jas. "Ozment did it."

The cab was filled with cheers and laughs of relief. The stomach-churning zigzagging of the truck ceased as Carl was able to keep it straight. He accelerated, quickly increasing the distance between them and the scene of carnage behind.

Jas scanned the dashboard screens and took a look out of the window at the night sky and the traffic that was beginning to fill the road around them again. It seemed there was no further pursuit. She hoped it would be a straight run now to the safety of Ozment's farm, and their next plan.

Suddenly she realized the Martian still hadn't climbed down.

Sayen had had the same thought. "Ozment's taking his

time." She leaned over the seats and called his name through the open hatch.

The missing man made no reply. Jas's heart sank. "Krat," she muttered, adding, "I'll check on him." She undid her seatbelt and climbed over Sayen to reach the hatch. Slotting her fingers and toes into the depressions in the tunnel, she climbed up.

The first thing she saw was the back of a low swivel chair and Ozment's arms and legs splayed out either side of it. Fighting the dread that rose up and threatened to over-whelm her, Jas climbed out into the narrow, low space. Ozment was seated behind a missile launcher. The roof above him had been retracted, and his position was open to the sky. An easy target from above, it was a suicidal spot.

The Martian was still alive, though from the state of his chest, he seemed to be holding on by willpower alone.

"Hey, Jas," he whispered.

She took his hand. "Hey, Ozment. You did a brave thing. You saved us."

"It was worth it." He smiled. "It was good to know you guys. Especially you, Jas. Good to see another Martian." He coughed. Blood ran from his mouth.

"I'm glad I met you, too." She couldn't say any more.

"Fight the fight, Jas. You know what I mean."

She gripped his hand tighter. Ozment looked up at the stars, and then he was gone.

Jas stayed for a while, wishing she'd had more time with him. They hadn't talked about Mars, or his life since coming to Earth, or his farm. There was so much she didn't know about this man who had given his life so nobly.

It was Sayen calling to her that broke her from her trance.

"I'm coming," she replied. She went down the tunnel

feet first and climbed out into the cab. The others seemed to tell from her face what had happened.

Only Makey needed confirmation. Very quietly, he asked, "He's gone?"

Jas nodded as she resumed her position by the window. No one spoke. From behind the seats came the sound of Erielle weeping.

Her face set, Jas looked out, unseeing, into the night.

18

They buried Ozment in the corner of a field next to a deserted farm track about a kilometer off the freeway.

Erielle managed to hobble from the truck to the burial spot on her crutches. She sank down to the ground next to the freshly filled grave and bent her head as if in silent prayer.

Jas wondered if she was commending Ozment's spirit to Earth Mother. She didn't really understand the beliefs of the underworlders. They seemed to be a very personal thing and something that had changed from the older to the younger generation.

"Jas, do you want to say anything?" Sayen asked.

She shook her head. "I'm no good at that stuff."

"I can recite the funeral rights they say on Dawn," said Makey. "I remember them."

"Okay," said Erielle. "I think he might have liked that."

Makey began, "Earth Mother, accept this man who is returning to you. Take his body as nourishment for living things. Return his soul to the natural spirits from where it came. Spread it wide, and let him delight in life once more, part of the whole which is you..."

Jas gazed down at the mound of crumbly soil, moister and darker than the surrounding ground. Ozment's grave was under a tree. She thought he would have liked it. She made a mental note of the place so that if anyone who knew him wanted to visit, she could tell them the spot. She bit her lip. He'd been so full of life, it hardly seemed possible that he was gone. And so young. He'd had so much more living to do.

As she mulled over these thoughts, a rage rose in her. The Shadows had taken yet another life. They had to be stopped. She would halt them in their tracks, and she would make them pay for every human being they'd killed.

She became aware of silence. Makey had finished speaking. She heaved a sigh. "I guess we should get back to the truck and decide what we're going to do next."

Sayen helped Erielle to her crutches, and the two left the graveside, followed by Carl and Makey. Jas was the last to leave. Before she went, she whispered, "Goodbye, friend."

CARL SAT behind the steering wheel of the parked truck with Makey next to him. Erielle was now well enough to join them on the seat. Sayen scooted over as Jas approached, making room for her next to the window.

"Where are we going?" Makey asked.

"I don't know yet," Jas replied. "I'm not sure that it's such a good idea to go to Ozment's farm. It's a safe hiding place, yes, but I don't think that hiding is what we should be doing right now. We have to contact the Transgalactic Council. We can't stop the Shadows without their help. We have to show them what's happening here."

"What is there on Ozment's farm, Erielle?" Sayen asked. "I'm guessing there isn't any kind of deep-space linkup?"

"I haven't been there for years," Erielle replied, "but, no, I don't think there's anything like that."

"All those places where you can send a deep-space comm are off limits to us," Carl said. "We don't have a krat's chance of breaking into any of those places. We don't have a Shadow as proof yet either."

"Hmmm...I'm not sure about that," Sayen said.

"You mean we do have a Shadow?" Jas asked.

"No, I meant about not having access to a deep space comm device."

"Really?"

"I'm pretty sure my parents send deep-space comms all the time."

"Then why haven't they told the Transgalactic Council about the Shadows?" Jas asked.

"They probably have, but for some reason they aren't being taken seriously."

"They did tell me and Carl about being shut out of meetings and having information withheld," Jas said. "You think we should go to your parents' place? They told us we couldn't go back there. That it wasn't safe."

"It doesn't seem very safe not to go there, though, does it?" said Sayen. "Think about it. We've got no creds and no place to go except Ozment's farm, which doesn't help us over the long term. How will we survive with only this truck? Heck, we don't even have the creds to pay for a battery recharge."

They had discussed removing Ozment's credchip, but they didn't have the equipment for inserting it into someone's wrist even if they'd been prepared to despoil his body, which they were not.

"My parents' house is damned near impregnable," Sayen continued. "If we can just get inside with a Shadow and contact the Council...I reckon it's our best option."

Jas wondered how much of Sayen's reasoning was influenced by her concerns for her mother and father, but she was making some good points.

"It's no good," Carl said. "If your parents are being watched by Shadows...if Shadows are surrounding the place, the minute we go near it they'll capture us. We'll never get in."

Sayen sighed. "Yeah, I guess you're right. I guess it was just wishful thinking."

"What about if your parents knew we were coming?" Erielle asked. "If they were ready for us? Could they fix things so that we could blast through the Shadows and drive right in?"

"Maybe, but we can't contact them," said Jas. "Sayen's parents warned us not to use anything that will allow us to be traced. The Shadows will instantly follow every comm her parents receive to its source. They'll swoop down on us and catch us."

"But if it were an anonymous message from a moving source?" Erielle asked.

"An anonymous..." Sayen's eyes widened. She touched the interface on the dashboard. "Ozment said this interface was untraceable. I used it to call your old doctor friend, and he couldn't see any caller ID."

"I doubt it's strictly untraceable," Erielle said. "Even our best isn't up to that. But the Shadows won't know who's calling, and they won't be able to see or hear the message. If you make the call while we're on the move, we'll be ten kilometers away before they figure out where it came from."

"It could work," Jas said to Sayen. "Your parents could tell us if they can get us inside their home. If they can, we don't even have to find a Shadow before we get there."

"Huh?" Carl said. "What good's it going to do to turn up at Sayen's parents' place without a Shadow?"

"I didn't say that," Jas replied. "If they're surrounding the place, they won't be hard to find. We can grab one on the way in."

Carl started up the truck. "I don't know if it'll work, but it's worth a try."

"I think so, too," Sayen said, smiling for the first time in days.

As they drove away from Ozment's grave, Jas watched it retreat into the distance. In her heart, she promised him that she wouldn't give up until she had defeated the Shadows and avenged his death.

'Fight the fight,' he'd said. She wondered what he'd meant. Something more than fighting the Shadows? He'd dedicated his life to struggling against the Global Government. Jas had never thought about them as a force for evil, but it was true that they were neglecting their duty to protect Earth's citizens. Had Ozment meant that they should fight them too? Had he meant that she should take up the underworlders' cause, perhaps following in the footsteps of her parents?

She turned to face forward. They were entering the freeway, and the open road stretched out before them. What the future held, Jas couldn't guess, but she wondered if it might somehow also lead back into her past.

JAS'S STORY CONTINUES IN…
TRAPPED

Shadows of the Void Book 7

Sign up to my reader group for a free copy of *Starbound*, the Shadows of the Void prequel that tells the story of what happened to Jas Harrington in Antarctica, and for exclusive notice of new releases, advanced reader opportunities and other interesting stuff:

https://jjgreenauthor.com/free-books/

(I won't send spam or pass on your details to a third party.)

www.ingramcontent.com/pod-product-compliance
Lightning Source LLC
Chambersburg PA
CBHW072145180726

48291CB00005BA/1632